I0831859

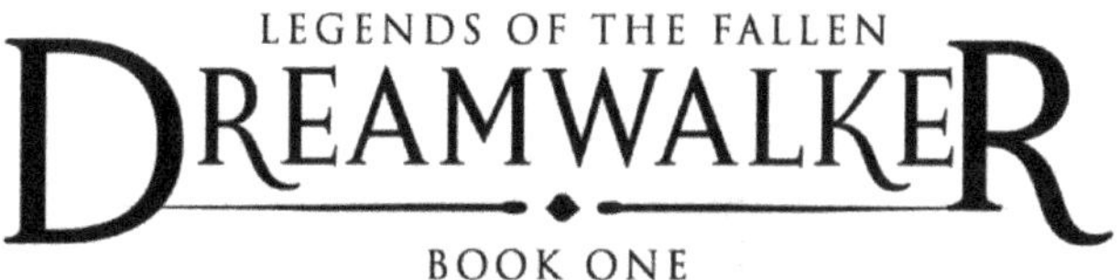

J.A. Culican

Tanya Dawson

ISBN-13978-1-949621-07-5

www.dragonrealmpress.com

Tanya Dawson's Dedication

I want to dedicate this book to my husband, Tyler. You're my biggest cheerleader and supporter. I'd also like to thank J.A. Culican for choosing me to be a part of this project and Frankie Blooding for helping me to become a better writer.

Audra
Desert of Souls
Bor'sur
Western March
Lower City
The Oubilee Desert
Prison
Blasted Lands
Bomrega Island
Dragon Dominion
Barren Wastes
Abrecem Secer
The Library
Cliffside
Caera
Low Forest (humans)
Low Forest (elves)
Great River Gethadrelle
Rilyo
Waterdeep
Bruhier
Lamruil
Thimmel
Southern Plains
Barepost
Havenport
Gleet
Lynia

CONTENTS

Chapter One 9
Chapter Two 21
Chapter Three 35
Chapter Four 47
Chapter Five 59
Chapter Six 73
Chapter Seven 83
Chapter Eight 95
Chapter Nine 105
Chapter Ten 117
Chapter Eleven 129
Chapter Twelve 143
Chapter Thirteen 155
Chapter Fourteen 169
Chapter Fifteen 181
Chapter Sixteen 193
Chapter Seventeen 205
Chapter Eighteen 217
Chapter Nineteen 231
Chapter Twenty 243
Chapter Twenty-One 255
Chapter Twenty-Two 267
Chapter Twenty-Three 281
Chapter Twenty-Four 293
Chapter Twenty-Five 307
Epilogue 319

Books by J.A. Culican 323
About the J.A. Culican 324
Contact J. A. Culican 325
About Tanya Dawson 325
Acknowledgements 325

"You can't hold me back forever." The gong had just rung, calling for reinforcements from our small town due to a skirmish.

And we had to sit here and prepare vegetables with the rest of the healers.

How could I be the only one who felt this was *wrong?*

"We have much to practice and learn." Mother Ofburg raised a dark eyebrow at me as she worked away, snapping the ends off the peas. "*Healing* is our contribution to our people."

It was easy for her to say. She'd been a healer for.... well, a long time. It wasn't natural for me. "What if I don't want to be like you?" I pointed at Noble, my best friend and fellow healer. "Or you?"

"One day, you will find peace and realize that you are a healer, not a fighter." Mother Ofburg poured her plate of beans into a sack we'd be giving to the farmers whose crops had died overnight.

I shut my mouth, knowing nothing I'd said would change her mind. Mother Ofburg was a respected healer and leader in our small town. I was one of three apprentices in her care and quite possibly the worst.

No. I *was* the worst. I had no idea why she kept trying with me. From my botched spells to the time I burned the outhouse down on a full moon by accident. Magic didn't flow through my veins. Fighting did.

The pounding of war drums thrilled me. I closed my eyes briefly for a moment, remembering my first time. My one and only fight.

The reason my parents sent me here.

I opened my eyes and glared at Mother Ofburg, a look so familiar to her she ignored it.

Her family had been healers for centuries. Her long grey hair was always pulled up in a bun, her face tanned and wrinkled from being outside. She pronounced every syllable slowly and clearly, so any misfit could understand.

I hated that. It made me feel slow.

Guilt washed over me as I slouched my shoulders in my seat. It was not Mother Ofburg's fault I'd ended up here.

I averted my gaze toward Noble. He kept his head down and worked around my drama. He was handsome enough but had sworn his life to healing. No women for him, not even the questionable girls in town. But they loved the challenge. He kept the sides of his head shaved, and the top long and pulled back in a ponytail. His bright green eyes could pierce anyone. His dimples were his most adoring feature.

"Are you done pouting?" Mother Ofburg poured the last of her beans into a bag.

I stood, grabbing the bag. "Noble?"

He snubbed me and poured his beans into his sack.

I stood there and studied him. Had he ever thought of me as more than a sister-figure? I was pretty enough. Had my fair share of men and women who'd shown interest in me, but I'd never managed to find the one. I wasn't thin like most girls. I practiced sword fighting in secret, deep in the woods, and it had kept me in good shape. My long auburn hair was the attribute I loved the most about myself. Though, my violet eyes drew the most attention.

"I'm ready." Noble headed to the door.

I grabbed my sack and moved to catch up with him. “Noble, wait.” I shut the large wooden door behind us.

There was not a lot of money in healing. That wasn’t the purpose of being a healer, so we lived like most of the townspeople. Our homes built into the hills, covered in moss and grass. Some buildings were made from wood, but they leaked. It was much better to use clay and hay to reinforce the walls. Building into the hills also allowed us to remain hidden to creatures flying above.

Like the ur’gel, demons from the northern deserts.

“We have to meet Skyra,” The tone of his voice was irritable. “She’ll lead us to the farmers that need us most.”

When we’d commenced our apprenticeships, we’d both felt like we’d belonged somewhere else. But then he’d given up. He’d *sworn* his *life* to healing. That.... sure felt like giving up to me. I don’t know why I thought he’d understand my need.

“I’m sorry. Okay?” I caught up to him and grabbed his hand. I forced my energy into his palm to prove it. As a healer, he would be able to feel my emotions just from touching the heat that rose from my body. Sharing our energy had bonded us, unlike any relationship before. It was impossible to lie to another healer.

He pushed my hand away and shook his head as he walked on.

"I just wanted—" I tried to get him to understand how frustration sometimes overtook my common sense, but perhaps I had gone too far this time.

His shoulders drooped.

In defeat? Was he angry?

"I understand why you're mad. I *don't* understand why you won't change the way you think." He stopped and faced me, his eyes watery.

My stomach dropped. How insensitive could I be? He'd sworn his life to healing when he lost three brothers in battle. His parents had sent him to Mother Ofburg to preserve his line by becoming a healer. He'd been a great warrior in his day, or so the rumors were. I would never ask him, though. Being a healer wasn't a step down by any means. It took many years of studying at the Healer's Guild in Abrecem Secer before you could even become an apprentice. Noble could have chosen to heal in the battlefield as a battle walker but chose to work in a village.

I held up my hands in surrender. “No more talk of it.” I smiled and punched his arm, then turned and ran.

Noble paused for a moment and then chased after me.

Like old times.

We ran giggling. He never caught me, although he could have without even breaking a sweat. We ran past the Millers, the Gates, the Burns, until we reached the edge of town. We fell onto the soft grass under a tree to catch our breath as we waited for Skyra.

The beauty of our town in the spring always brought a smile to my face. The snow had melted, and all Rilyo’s bounties were in the process of growing again. The town itself was large and shared with humans and elves. We all tried to get along, but raiding occurred. While I liked the town and its people, I wouldn’t be here forever. The ache in my soul said otherwise.

“Can we just ban talking about fighting?” He leaned back on the grass and stretched.

“This isn’t going to be my life.” I lay next to him on my side. I thought of him as a brother but could appreciate his beauty.

“It’s better than dying.” He shifted his body so he faced me. His large hand reached toward my face to lift away the stray hairs that had fallen into my eyes.

“We can all die at any time.” I was grateful for his touch. Not being with family had left me hungry for hugs and physical comfort.

Noble didn’t respond. Instead, his gaze was distant.

Would he ever talk about them with me?

Probably not. “But today we feed the hungry.” I smiled at him, then flopped back on my back. Skyra wouldn’t be long. I wanted to soak in every second of not having to do anything but wait.

“Skyra is late. For once, I’m happy about that.” He smiled and joined me again, lying on his back.

We lay in silence, enjoying the soft breeze, smelling the blossoming flowers and calm in the woods. It was so peaceful we almost fell asleep.

We sensed Skyra’s energy before we caught sight of her. She was not only a bundle of energy but also the tallest person in town. An awkward combo.

“Wakey, wakey!” Skyra pounced on the ground at our feet.

Skyra worked for the Council Three. They ruled the Low Forest, and we often did work for them.

They were investigating the crop failure. She had just won a leadership tournament and was now one of the most popular guides. There was something about her which made you want her on your side. I often confided in her and respected her opinion. She understood me.

"You're late." Noble rose to his feet in one leap.

"Come on, slackers. We have adventuring to do." Skyra headed into the woods, and we followed.

"So, what are we walking into?" We'd only heard the rumors and questioned if it was as bad as it had been made out to be. What could destroy entire crops in one night?

"We're coming up on the first farm." Skyra crouched down and extended her arms out to stop us. She brought her finger to her lips, instructing us to remain quiet.

She removed the bow from her hip and notched an arrow.

I tried to see what she did. There was nothing there.

Noble's eyes fixed on a spot ahead of us.

I leaned over and saw the branches move. What was it? A bandit? An animal?

A deer shot out.

Skyra released her arrow, and the deer fell to the ground. She moved to it and placed her hands on the animal, offering up the hunting prayers and ensuring it wasn't suffering. Moments later, she swung the deer over her shoulder, and we moved on.

"Beatrice will be thankful. Her crops were hit the worst." She carried the heavy deer with ease as we came across a clearing.

I stopped in my tracks, the view shocking. The field was filled with black soot. "Did it burn?"

"No. We have no idea what this is, and it just keeps growing." Skyra headed toward the clay home.

I couldn't even begin to imagine the devastation. "Beatrice Mulligan. We went to school together. Her father was killed in the war." Her mother had found comfort elsewhere, but I kept that part to myself.

"She's married now." Skyra knocked on the door. "Happily, with child, and they have their own farm elsewhere. It's safe for now." After several moments, and no answer, she placed the deer next to the door. "Follow me."

She walked past the small house to a wooden building.

"Anyone here?" Skyra yelled into the barn.

“Up here,” a man called back as he came down the ladder to greet us.

“Came to look things over.” Skyra stepped inside.

“You got those healers with you?”

Another thing I hated. People never used our names.

“Yup.”

He set his pitchfork on the platform and leaned on it, looking at us. But he talked to Skyra even though we stood right there. “Mother Ofburg sent a boy looking for ‘em. They’re needed back right away.”

“I’ll get them there. You safe here? I brought your family meat.”

“I’ll never turn down meat. These old bones don’t get to hunt very often. Thank you for the offering.”

Skyra turned toward us and motioned with her head to follow her through the woods again.

We were quick on her tail. Worry gnawed at me. Some of our fighters had gone out. She was calling us back in. That meant there must be wounded members.

“I hope she’s ok.”

“The skirmish destroyed people and land,” Skyra shouted over her shoulder. “Multiple dead.”

“Where did it happen?” Noble’s voice was uneasy.

“Choked Valley.”

The muscles in Noble’s neck stiffened.

His hometown.

His pace picked up, and I tried my best to match it.

From my guess, it had been three years since he’d been back, even though it was not far.

“I hear you still want to fight?” Skyra changed the subject

It was not something I wanted the Council Three to know about. But I couldn’t lie to her. “I’m thinking about it.”

She snorted as we reached the edge of the woods outside Choked Valley.

As I looked down the stretch of land, the smoke from the charred trees and the burned houses irritated my nostrils. Few homes still stood, and those that did were badly damaged.

"Stick with your apprenticeship. You don't want to see what I have to. You're both on your own now. I'll take care of the deliveries. Good luck"

We handed off our bags, eager to see the damage and destruction up close. Being a warrior was difficult, fighting every battle no questions asked, wondering who would make it back and who wouldn't.

Skyra disappeared back into the woods.

Noble and I shared a look, then we both took off running toward the village. This time, he beat me. I was at least ten minutes longer getting back.

As soon as I entered the town square, my eyes were drawn to Noble, who was now on the ground, hugging his mother. Having never seen him cry before, I clutched my stomach with my shaky hands.

My anger stirred inside of me, and I never wanted to fight more. But for now, I had to stay and help heal these people. Right then and there, I vowed to myself I would avenge Noble and his family.

The wounded finally stopped arriving. I went from patient to patient, healing the best I could, and tried to keep Noble and his family out of my thoughts. The images of them in pain made it difficult for me to concentrate. As did the many people I'd seen every day that were arriving with varying degrees of injury from the skirmish. With the number of injuries, it was difficult to believe we had won the battle.

Mother Ofburg worked as triage, sorting the injured by their wounds. I tended to the least severe since I was the least adept healer in her apprenticeship. I worked fast with my hands to heal scrapes, bruises, and the odd broken bone.

A hand on my back startled me. Noble stood over me. He didn't look great.

"I need to see you."

I finished with my patient and picked up my first aid bag. I pushed my emotions deep inside me where I could burn them as fuel.

"How is your mother?"

"She'll be ok." He grabbed my hand and pulled me outside.

He was pale, not white pale, more greyish, and sweat rolled down his face.

My jaw clenched in fear of what he could reveal to me. I'd never seen him like this before.

"We won, but barely. Some of our villagers are saying it's one of the great monsters." The corners of his lips pulled down.

The ur'gel. They were dark monsters that were whispered about in stories. What was he thinking? The ur'gel lived far from here. They lived in the north.

"Are you sure? You know how things often get told." I tried my best to see if I could calm him.

"The way they describe them...." Noble trailed off as he searched for the right words. "It has to be the ur'gel."

"Why would they travel this far?" He was looking for an excuse for what had happened to his mother. He wasn't thinking straight.

"There's something people don't know about the ur'gel," his voice ragged. "Over time, they mixed with different races, and the creatures that the old gods created are not the same as the fairy tales. I've *seen* them in battle. These are the same wounds. A thick cut with a jagged edge." Noble looked back at the injured.

"Should I talk to the Council Three?" I was confused and unsure if I should believe him. It was unlikely the ur'gel had arrived this far south. The fear was always there, but the ur'gel hadn't been this far south in over two hundred years. So why would they start now?

"Let's keep tending to the injured." Noble's eyes were wide and glazed. "I have to think about how to handle this without scaring everyone. This could mean bad things. We need to handle it a certain way."

He was standing in front of me in body only. I didn't know what to do for him. Once things calmed down, I would try to talk to him again. Hopefully after a good sleep, he'd snap out of his daze and this would be something we could laugh at in a couple of years.

Noble and I went our separate ways back to our stations to begin healing again. The work was daunting, stealing energy from our bodies. As the injured dwindled down, Mother Ofburg told me to return home for the evening, to be with my family. She took Noble by the arm when she'd dismissed me, a sadness showing on her face as if she didn't know what to do for him either.

It had been about a week since I had been home, and for the first time, I was excited to go. I needed things to at least appear normal.

I took one of the horses we kept on reserve for healing and headed to our homestead on the opposite side of Rilyo, taking as many shortcuts as I could to get home.

As I came through the clearing, the site of the small house with smoke rising from the chimney immediately called for me. It was difficult to remember why I stayed away so often.

When I opened the door, the small room was crammed with my parents, brothers, and some of their family waiting for me with a full harvest meal. Everyone was there for me.

I first noticed a very pregnant Vinsha, my oldest brother Damour's wife, and they had never seemed happier.

"About time you showed up." Damour rubbed my head, ruffling my hair like I was still a little kid.

"I came as soon as I could." My voice lowered. For just a second, seeing everyone together made me forget the pain from the past couple of days.

"We get it." Damour's voice was forgiving.

Raiding had been something we'd had to deal with over the years, but they'd killed more people in the past few raids. Damour lost his young shop boy just a few weeks ago.

"My daughter is home after a round of healing people." Mother squeezed me tightly as she held back tears. She pulled back from me, and we both shared a look. She knew I needed to be here, and she wasn't going to ask any questions.

"Gavin." I squealed as I ran toward him and knelt as I wrapped my arms around his body, careful not to topple over his wheelchair. It still pained me to see him in that chair after all these years. One stupid mistake because of childhood arrogance and a lifetime to pay for playing around with magic.

"I missed you." Gavin squeezed around me weakly. As I pulled back from him, something had changed, and it made me feel a little queasy.

"Let your best-looking brother give you a hug," Denny called from behind me.

I was about to face him as he hugged around my waist and swung me around. He was well built from working the farm from sun up to sun down. His long blond tail whipped about as we almost fell over.

"Let me down!"

"Say it!"

"Never." I giggled.

"That's enough, children," my father interrupted our play.

Before I could say anything, he led me to the table. "Only the best seat in the house for our daughter." He sat me at the head of the table.

I grimaced, knowing how much of a failure I had been to them. This special treatment was likely the result of the gossip about the raids and healing I had done.

It had been too long since all of us were under the same roof. But there was always one missing. My brother, Harov, had moved out without saying goodbye. Since then, everything had changed. With each of us losing friends in these raids, we were thankful we still had most of our loved ones left unharmed.

"It is always a good day when my children are together." My mother stood with a proud, strong expression on her face, opposite of her frail body and hunched back.

"It's good to be home." Though it also felt weird to be here under the circumstances.

"Let's revel in today. Now, let's all eat up." Mother raised her glass.

"There's talk about the skirmish." Damour settled in to eat. "The numbers were rather large this time."

"We won, which is the main point." I somehow doubted that.

"Just barely."

"You weren't there." His tone irked me. He'd never *been* in battle.

"No, thank goodness, I was not." Damour was unapologetic.

Mother gripped her spoon. "There will be no discussions of fighting at this table."

She never liked discussing difficult topics.

"I've heard the old Greys no longer have an outhouse." Gavin exchanged a glance with me, laughing to try and break the thick mood that had settled around the table.

I could count on him to make me laugh when I thought it wasn't possible. I needed to laugh right now, to not see the injured every time I closed my eyes.

"It was old and shabby anyways." I smiled back at him. He was not in favor of me becoming a healer.

He'd wanted me to be a fighter, and he knew that was all I ever wanted to be.

"We need to let Aria rest. I imagine she's had a very rough day today." Father gave us all a stern look.

How I missed that look. It reminded me of simpler times when staying out late was the worst thing I could do.

We finished our meal, and my brothers helped clean up the dishes while my parents and I sat by the fire.

"I'm proud of you." My father reached over and rubbed my arm.

They were words I once thought I'd never hear from my father. I had only given them one disappointment after another.

I'd missed our late-night discussions and stories about his youth and his fighting days. We weren't allowed to discuss them in front of Mother, but he shared my love for fighting. He had been the one that had told me about the Dark War and how the ur'gel were created. The stories had been passed down from generation to generation. Dag'draath had tried to conquer the world more than two hundred and fifty years ago and had been vanquished. He'd planted the seed of distrust in the hearts of all who survived, and since that time dragons, humans, and elves had never gotten along. These stories had been special between us.

"I know I've not said that many times." He rocked in his chair as he fiddled with his hands.

"There were lots of times when you couldn't say it." I flattened my hands over my legs, not wanting to copy him. Something he had passed on to me when I was uncomfortable.

"Don't frighten her away." My mother gave a gentle push to my father and smiled at both of us.

"It's just been very tiring." I wiped my eyes.

"It's not easy being the one who solves problems."

"I can't stop thinking it. Especially the children."

Mother hugged me. "You'll do just fine. Take it one day at a time. If you can't, then one hour at a time."

I hadn't thought I had a tear left in me, but I could hardly explain away the water running down my cheeks. "I think I just need some time to rest."

"Then you must sleep, my child, please." My mother pointed toward their bedroom, the one good bed in the small house. Our beds were made from straw.

"I can't." I shook my head at my mother as she stood and directed me from the floor into the room.

"We'll take your bed. You need a good rest. I'll close the curtain and make sure the noise is kept down."

I didn't argue with her as I rubbed my burning eyes. I desperately needed to sleep.

She kissed my forehead, and then pulled the curtain closed.

I turned toward the bed and took off my shoes. The murmurs in the kitchen were like a sweet song.

It didn't take me long to fall asleep. The aches and pains of my body simply drifted away as I sank into the bed.

Reality mixed with dreams.

***

The land of living trees and plants had all died. The sky was dark without a sun. The ground was moist with a very unpleasant smell. My feet were firmly planted in the mud, without any wiggle room. I knew where I was, but how could it be? The Barren Wastes?

There was someone far in the distance. I called out to him, but it was as if he couldn't hear me. I began to walk toward him as I dragged my feet in the mud, then suddenly it was like something took over my body, and it was forcing me toward the stranger. He turned around and saw me. The look on his face was pure agony. His hands reached out to me, and a surge of energy connected me to him.

I felt his pain, and it was shocking. His anger at his condition shook me to my core as the sensation terrified me. Someone had hurt him. They wanted him to die.

He wasn't handsome. He had rugged features and was tattooed with many battle awards. His body was muscular yet thin from lack of food. His wrist showed signs of detainment, and his body was covered in dirt and blood.

I tried to get to him faster, but there was no sun, moon, or stars—just darkness. As I got closer to him, I could see another large figure walk toward us. I began to feel frightened, but I wasn't sure why. Everything began to happen in slow motion. I knew what was going to happen to the man, but I couldn't move anymore. I couldn't help him.

In the distance, an ur'gel grew closer. I wanted to scream out to warn him, but he stood there, staring at me. His eyes welled with tears as if he had been waiting for me for an exceptionally long time. I felt like I had been waiting for this moment as well.

As our eyes connected, I felt his pain, his fear, his wants. Tears flowed from my eyes as the pain in my heart became almost unbearable. I needed to get him out.

I was unable to do anything as the ur'gel attacked the man. The fight was intense and life-giving. The man tried his best. However, he was very weak, yet he blocked every attempt. The ur'gel swung at him fiercely, and the man avoided his sword by mere inches each time. My body shook in frustration. I wanted to run to him, but I was stuck in the mud, still unable to move.

The tip of the sword swiped the man on his side and pierced his skin. It was only a flesh wound, and if I could only get to him, I could heal him. I tried with everything I had inside of me to move. I lifted one foot. I squealed in delight, and the man looked my way. The ur'gel saw his window of opportunity and raised his sword, bringing it down, cutting into the man's hand.

I felt the most excruciating pain in my left hand. My gaze dropped to my left, and all I saw was blood. Panicked, I glanced back to the man and saw him on the ground, his hand reaching toward me . . .

A scream shot through my head.

I sat up, shaking with fear.

The scream had been mine.

I was light-headed and felt wet. I looked down at the sheets, and they were covered in blood.

How had I hurt my hand? In the dream? That didn't even make sense. I must have hit it on something while I had that dream. *That* made sense.

But that was a lie. I wished more than anything that it was all just a dream.

That he was okay.

That it wasn't real.

But it was real.

I pushed my thoughts far away and got ready for work. I hid my injured hand from my parents and my brothers the best I could. They'd worry about me, and I didn't dare tell them about my dream. I wrapped my hand and squeezed it into my leather glove. It throbbed, and I cringed at the pain. I just had to make it to the door.

I placed my hand over the wound and forced as much energy as I could into it, but the cut was too deep. I'd ask Noble for his help as soon as I returned to Mother Ofburg's.

Damour was in the kitchen when I peeked out of the bedroom, making breakfast. I pulled the curtain back, not wanting him to realize I'd awakened. I walked quietly toward the front door and touched the doorknob, hoping for a quick getaway.

"Aria," Damour's gravelly voice called, "where are you sneaking off to?"

"I didn't want to wake anyone." My stomach grumbled at the smell of pig bits being cooked, and it won out over the throbbing pain in my hand. I walked over to the pan and grabbed a few bits, then turned back toward the door.

"They didn't want to wake *you*, so they went out to pull some corn for later today." Damour turned his attention back to cooking but the hint of annoyance in his voice lingered.

"What's your problem?"

"You."

"Me?"

"The way you prance in here, expecting whatever you want. Head of the table, the best bed."

"I didn't ask for either of those things."

"You didn't turn them down either."

Damour never had a problem calling me out. He thought I was spoiled being the only girl in the family. But I wasn't about to feel guilty. Luckily, he was never hard-core about it.

"You're almost ready to be a dad." I smiled at the thought and sat down at the end of the table, facing him.

"It's something I've always wanted." Damour stirred the pot. "That's why I know how Mom and Dad feel. They need to be tougher on you."

My face flushed with embarrassment. He was right. I needed to get over the resentment I had for them pushing me into being a healer.

"And this fighting thing? It's over, right?" Damour's expression challenged me to respond.

"No fighting."

"I made yours to go." He nodded to a bowl wrapped in leather. "I figured you would eat on the way to work." His attention diverted back to the steaming pot.

"Thank you." I got up and almost used my left hand to push myself up. My legs wobbled in anticipation of the potential pain I just avoided.

I grabbed the bowl, giving him a peck on the cheek before heading to the door. It swung open, and Mother, Father, and Denny walked in.

"Are you leaving already?" Mother hugged me for a brief moment, then continued into the house.

"I'm sorry. I overslept. I've got to get back to Mother Ofburg to see what I can do to help." I moved to slip through the door.

"She will be needing all the help that she can get."

I hugged my father and nodded at Denny who was already at the table stuffing his face with food.

"Where's Gavin?" I didn't want to leave without seeing him.

"Not far behind us." Denny's arm flung out and pointed toward the door as he spoke around a mouthful of food.

The sun hit my face and brought on an immediate smile. I loved this land and the peace that came with it.

A shriek coming from the barn startled me, followed by a few curse words. I glanced toward my horse, and for a mere second debated jumping on and pretending I didn't hear anything. I shook my head and headed to the barn, wondering what stupid thing Gavin had done now.

As I entered the barn, Gavin sat in his wheelchair with broken glass all around him

"Gavin." I chuckled as I came up to him. "What are you doing?"

"Don't bring any more attention. I don't want the prying ears to find out." Gavin leaned over in his chair as he grabbed the glass.

He was practicing magic again.

"A spell?" I knelt over to help pick up the glass.

"I may have found a way." Gavin shifted his head from side to side as if he was debating on how much he could trust me with. "You can't tell anyone. Promise me."

"I promise." I stooped in front of him, waiting for him to tell me more.

"Something just happened to come to me by some means."

I rolled my eyes at the thought of him keeping a secret from me, especially with how many things we kept hidden from everyone over the years. "What is it, and where did you get it?"

"It was given to me, but I can't tell you from who, and don't think you can pressure me to tell you. I don't even know if it will work." He pulled at the wheels of his chair and moved past me.

I stood. Perhaps I could help him with what I had learned from Mother Ofburg. "I can help." I followed him out of the barn.

"No. You can't get involved."

"But I can help more now." Goosebumps tickled my arms at the thought of Gavin not being able to trust me.

"No. You need to act like you know nothing. That's how you can help me." Gavin's cheeks flushed, and his jaw tightened.

I nodded in agreement. It still bothered me he wouldn't share this new development, and it was all because I was too busy with my apprenticeship. I hadn't thought he would hold that against me.

"I know nothing." The thought of our close bond not being there hurt.

"One day I will tell you everything. I promise." Gavin threw some hay at me with a devilish grin.

"Deal." We both linked our thumbs together in our secret code.

"Now, you better get off to work, because I hear that Mother Ofburg can be something fierce." He smiled almost like he loved the idea of me getting into trouble.

I leaned over and hugged him. "See you, little one." I ruffled his hair and ran off before he could grab my hand. "Gotcha."

He swung his arms out to catch me, but I was too quick.

I ran at a steady pace and managed to get up on my horse without hurting my hand more. The ride back to Mother Ofburg's healing hut in Rilyo took longer, and each pounce of the horse made my hand throb. I had never been so happy to see that little hut.

As soon as my feet hit the ground, I made my way to find Noble. He was still in the hut tending to the wounded, which seemed to be dwindling. When we made eye contact, he dismissed himself from his case and walked over to me.

"How is your mother doing?"

"Better. She'll make a full recovery."

"What's wrong?" He grabbed my arms and I winced.

I lifted my gloved hand. It was twice the size of my other.

He slipped his hand under my elbow and guided me to a room off the main hall. "How'd this happen?" He skillfully cut the glove off in one swipe.

"On the farm. I was stupid. Not paying attention." I held my breath as the pain intensified as my hand throbbed.

Noble brought my hand up to his face to examine the wound.

"This is not a farm wound. It's from an ur'gel sword. You promised me you wouldn't go off and fight." He pressed his lips together and frowned.

"Can you help me?" I didn't want to go to Mother Ofburg for help. She would demand to know the full story.

He pointed at a chair for me to sit down in.

I obeyed. The less talking, the better.

He brought over a bowl and placed my hand into it. He stepped out of the room and, a few moments later, returned with a bucket of hot water.

"We have to disinfect first." Noble mixed some cooler water in with the hot. He poured the water into the bowl, and my hand became submerged. It stung and burned. I sat still and didn't move. I just wanted this over with. Every time I closed my eyes, the man from the dream reached for me.

Noble waved his hand over the bowl and tried to use his energy to heal me, but nothing happened. He grabbed a pouch under his fur throw and pulled out some small green plant with stiff spikes. He squeezed the leaf, and the gel dripped onto my wound. Next, he pulled on several medical drawers until he found a bottle, a few drops of wolf oil to activate the gel, but again, nothing happened.

Noble sat back for a moment as his eyes darted back and forth as he flipped through one of our healing books. He stood and opened a few drawers and mixed a concoction of herbs and applied them as a paste to my wound. After twenty minutes of waiting, he removed the paste, but the wound had more puss.

“It’s not good.” Noble murmured to himself as he paced the room. “I have one thing left.” He left the room.

I sat in silence as I waited for his return. I was getting groggy but feared going to sleep in case I went back into that horrible dream.

“Where is she?” Mother Ofburg’s voice grew louder as they got closer to the door.

I jumped off my chair and looked for an exit, but there wasn’t even a window in the little room.

“In here. I made sure she’s away from the rest of them,” I heard Noble’s voice.

"Aria. Is this true, what Noble has told me?" Mother Ofburg's voice was calm, the opposite of the look on her face.

"I didn't fight. I bumped my hand on something while I slept." I was practically tongue-tied as I tried to get the words out of my mouth. Why weren't they fixing it? Who cared how it happened?

"You were asleep when this happened?" Mother Ofburg's face grew curious.

"Just a clumsy move," I averted my eyes, not because they were right but because I knew they wouldn't believe me.

"There was an ur'gel in your dream?" Mother Ofburg asked diligently.

The look of shock on my face told her the answer. How did she know that?

She reached for my hand and turned it over to the wound. "This happened when you were dreamwalking."

"I can't dreamwalk." I half laughed at her suggestion.

"The healing gift that you have shouldn't be played with." Mother Ofburg tugged a little hard on my hand.

“What does dreamwalking have to do with healing? And it’s news to me that I can dreamwalk. Shouldn’t you be trying to teach me how to use it?” If she knew I had the potential to dreamwalk, why hadn’t she told me?

“You weren’t ready.” Mother Ofburg shook her head as she untied some bandages. Her hands shook as she tried to pull an end free. After about a minute, she threw them to the ground. “You never listen, and you don’t take anything seriously.”

I sat still.

“Bring me some calendula and comfrey. Make a paste with witch hazel and bring to boil. We don’t have much time before this infection spreads,” Mother Ofburg said to Noble, and he left the room.

“I promised your parents I would keep you out of trouble.”

I slouched lower in my seat, ready for whatever punishment she would give me.

Noble entered the room with a bowl and the ingredients she had asked for.

Mother Ofburg tended to me. It took a while, but my wound finally responded to one of their potions.

“Thank you. I’m sorry that I haven’t been as attentive as I should. I’m going to try harder.”

"They're here." Someone yelled in the main hall. Then people ran past the room we were in, screaming, heading toward the door.

Mother Ofburg, Noble, and I made our way out to them. We stayed against the wall, to not get trampled.

"What's happening?" Noble called out into the crowd, but no one stopped.

Noble grabbed one of the farmers who tried to run past us and picked him up off his feet to stop him. "Where is everyone going?"

"They're here! They're here! The ur'gel. They've come for their revenge." The man's voice was shaky, and his hands wouldn't stay still.

Noble placed him on the ground, and we all followed the farmers as they tried to get out of the hall.

The sight before us was total chaos, bloodied bodies on the ground and large monsters swiftly killing the village people with their swords. We were indeed under attack.

I ran to the little barn behind the hut, my hands steady as the adrenaline rushed through my veins. No one would take over my town. I grabbed a bow as my weapon of choice. The spear would be my backup and for closer encounters.

I held the spear over my head and thrust it toward the ground to get my grip just right. My bow leaned against the wall with a quiver of arrows nearby. Everything was in check. How I wished I had my good bow, the one Gavin and I made me from a rare Antear tree, but that was at home, hidden.

Without hesitation, I ran toward the fighting. I found a good location where I could attack from the side. I used the hay bales left out for the horses as a base and prayed to whatever god was listening the ur'gel hadn't yet seen me. I'd only have a split second to do damage before they spotted my location and tried to end my life.

I spread my feet apart, shoulder width, and exhaled as I lifted my bow in front of me. I relaxed my hand and pulled back on the bowstring. The string tickled my nose as I aimed down the arrow at my first ur'gel. Releasing the bowstring, I held my breath in anticipation as my arrow punctured the ur'gel through the back of the head.

The ur'gel fell to the ground in a bloody heap, dead. I scanned for my next target, reminding myself to keep my cool as I didn't want any false hope in clearing out these monsters.

I notched another arrow in place. The arrow released, and I missed my target, which pulled me back to reality. I had to be accurate. I didn't have time to think. I lifted my head and tried to gauge how many monsters were attacking. I observed at least twenty. Why were they here?

The local baker took out an ur'gel with a knife to the eye.

The blacksmith stuck a very hot iron in as many monsters as he could, but his rod wouldn't stay hot for long.

A seven-foot ur'gel approached him from behind, I steadied my bow and took a shot, missing by inches. I released a second one, and it grazed the side of the ur'gel's cheek.

"Aria! Behind you," a male voice said.

I flipped around and saw an ur'gel running toward me. I grabbed my spear, aiming for his gut. I pushed off and watched it land in his chest. Not my target, but it'd do. His large body fell to the ground.

I yanked the spear, but it wouldn't budge. I tried again, placing my foot on the dead monster, and heaving with all my weight to pull it out. It moved with a crack and came out minus the tip.

"Are you all right?" Noble came to stand beside me.

I didn't have time to respond. The monsters just kept coming. It was impossible to even determine how many at this point. Village people ran, trying to hide, while others took whatever they could and battled for their lives.

One woman threw books from her front door at anything that bothered to come near. Another man set fire to hay and threw it at the ur'gel.

The persistence to defeat these attackers burrowed in our hearts and souls. People who had never fought before attacked the monsters as bravely as they could, fighting them with anything within hand's reach.

I grabbed my bow and readied it, aiming it at the closest monster to me. The options were plentiful, and I couldn't risk missing and hitting someone instead of a monster.

Noble gave my arm a shake and headed into the deep of it. I marveled to see him swing his sword and put down whatever monster was in his way. Noble the Warrior.

I jumped over my fort and entered the fight. At first, I'd been able to clear a path, and a few village people surrounded me. We worked together. My arrow reserve was getting low. I needed to make them count. I had three left. Then I would need to rely on my broken spear.

My first arrow made a kill. The second missed and made the ur'gel furious at my attempt. He came thrashing my way.

The sweat from my forehead stung my eyes as I reached for my last arrow. I hesitated and shot my arrow and hit him in the thigh. I reached back for my broken spear.

The monster ran toward me. I crouched low to the ground to swing my spear upward as he approached.

He grabbed it and slammed me to the ground, causing me to lose my breath.

I was not going to make this, but I wouldn't die a coward.

He brought his spear just over his head.

I had to get the timing right. As he swung down, I rolled between his legs and ran as fast as I could to hide by the hut until I could get another resource to use. The ur'gel wasn't too smart and spent some time swinging his arms about as he looked for me.

"You're lucky he's got half a brain," someone said from behind me, startling me.

"Sade." Thank goodness. I had dreamed of fighting alongside Sade Lemm, and now it was actually happening.

Sade was a monster hunter, the most skilled slayer around. She followed them and then killed them, alone I may add. She made grown men cry just by giving them a saucy look. She became a monster hunter when her entire family had been murdered by vampires. People taunted her for running away that night, being a white wolf. Now she was respected and paid very well to keep the monsters at bay.

"Here." She handed me some of her arrows. "You're not a bad shot. Pace the breathing and take the extra second you need."

I grabbed the arrows from her hand, trying to act nonchalantly about working side by side with her.

"Stay behind me." She moved forward.

I stayed close to her side and shot at anything coming our way. Each arrow she pulled hit its target. She repeated the same action five times, not missing her marks, before I had readied my arrow.

"That's amazing."

"You see that man over there?" Sade pointed to a body on the ground.

I nodded my head.

"This isn't a game, kid."

I could feel my cheeks burn at my childishness. I'd never be a great warrior like Noble or Sade.

Sade reached over and lifted my chin so our eyes were level. "It's in you. Don't let arrogance steal the warrior inside." She pounded two fingers into my chest at the rhythm of a heartbeat.

A sudden burst of energy filled me, and I was ready to fight.

Sade nodded for me to go right as she went left. I pulled my arrow out and placed it on the shelf of the arrow rest, aimed the arrow, took a large breath, and on my exhale, let the arrow fly.

A shot just to the left of the chest. I wouldn't let myself smile at or relish the moment. I went on and shot six more, all missing their targets.

"Aria!" a male voice shouted.

I turned my head as an ax swung by and scraped my cheek.

Noble swung his spear right into the monster that attacked me.

We took cover and caught our breath.

"Are you okay?" Noble reached for my face to inspect my wound.

"I'm fine." I pushed his hand away. I didn't want to be babied. I could take care of myself just fine.

"Go to Mother Ofburg. Help her shield the weak ones from the ur'gel."

"I'm no use there." I belonged in the fighting. I turned from him and headed back into battle.

Bloodied bodies of humans and monsters lay intertwined.

The ur'gel kept coming, no matter how many we killed. I focused on what my next target should be.

"Back from your nap, kid?" Sade arrived beside me, her sleeve ripped and bloodied.

"Are you all right?"

"Just a warrior wound. Go for the blue ones. They tend to be slower. You'll go further with your arrows." Sade reached down and counted the arrows that I had left—five. She had run out of her arrows and had already ditched her bow. She had a spear in one hand and a small knife for upfront combat in the other.

I nodded at her advice. Then she took off running and screaming into the town, hacking at the ur'gel. She made herself the target to help me. I couldn't help but wonder if Sade would be the last person I ever spoke to.

I readied my bow and peeked over the barricades to look for blue ur'gel. I spotted one about to attack the baker's son and shot an arrow through its left arm. While the ur'gel tried to pull it out, the man was able to get away.

I reached to grab another arrow, keeping my eye on my next target. My hand searched the ground, but all I could feel was grass. I turned to see where my arrows disappeared to.

An ur'gel stood behind me with what little arrows I had left in his hands. He snapped them over his knee. Then he removed his sword from his side and slammed it toward me.

A quick roll to the right saved me, but he was quicker. His hand grabbed my jacket and lifted me up. He had to be at least eight feet tall.

I flailed my feet, hoping to knock him off balance.

"Noble!" He was out of sight—out of earshot. The ur'gel flung me back, and I hit the ground, knocking the wind out of me.

His large fist with small knives attached to his knuckles crashed beside me, first left, then right, taunting my death.

This wasn't how I'd envisioned being a fighter would be. An ur'gel ending my life. I needed to fight back.

I gathered my energy and, with one leap, flipped back onto my feet. Now upright, I felt better than I had a few moments ago.

The ur'gel growled and swung his big hands.

I stepped back but not quickly enough. He elbowed me in the face, and again, I crumbled to the ground, this time coughing up blood.

A spear was only a few feet in front of me. I made a leap for it and landed with the spear under my hand. I turned around as he lunged toward me. I squeezed my eyes shut in anticipation of the spear slicing through the ur'gel's belly. Instead, the spear clashed with some sort of amour with a clang of metal.

What kind of ur'gel was this? I rolled over again, missing his next hit, as his fist smashed against the dirt where my head used to be. I needed to be able to get to my feet. I could make a run for it. I tried my best, but he grabbed my foot and pulled me back toward him. I was his toy.

"Leave me alone." I dangled in the air in front of the ur'gel. I flailed my arms around, trying to knock myself free, when I remembered I had bits of pepper in my pouch for my soup. I grabbed the little bit I had and aimed for his eyes.

The ur'gel dropped me to the ground as he rubbed his eyes. I scrambled to my feet and took off running. I didn't dare look back. I ran as fast as I could until my breathing became shallow. I ran to the blacksmith shop and entered through the cracked door. The windows were broken, the once-immaculate shop in disarray. I leaned over the anvil and tried to catch my breath. My chest was killing me. I was covered in blood, and I wasn't sure it was all mine.

A large hand grabbed my shoulder and pulled me backward. The ur'gel had already found me again. Before I could think of anything to do, he lifted me up and threw me clear across the room. I hit a cabinet full of irons and fell to the ground. My body ached all over. I was in so much pain I didn't know where it was coming from. This was the end.

I heard him as he walked toward me. Each big foot crumbled whatever it walked over. He'd be here any second. I couldn't move. My vision blurred to black, and I knew I was going to die, his face last thing I'd have seen in Low Forest.

He leaned over me and knelt down. His breath made my eyes water. I managed to turn my head away from him. I closed my eyes and prayed for a quick end.

Nothing happened.

I opened my eyes again, and somehow, I was home. I stood next to the barn, which was on fire. My worst fear was coming true. My family was being attacked.

My blood vessels hammered in my head, my heart pounded in my chest, and my ears heard no sounds. It took me a second to readjust, then I ran toward my hidden bow to retrieve it.

I was exhausted and tired. Now I had to pull off a miracle to protect my family. They were farmers. Not fighters.

My legs moved much slower than I anticipated, but I made it to the barn without being seen. I dug through the hay as the straw poked and scratched my hands and arms. With each move, pain struck my body in a different way.

I found my bow and quiver of arrows and planted myself in the loft by the window. I surveyed the land and the attackers. I recognized some of the monsters from town. They must have followed me home. However I got here.

My eyes closed in on an ur'gel who had a knife stuck in his armpit, courtesy of the local baker. It didn't faze him in any way. He walked toward the house. I grabbed an arrow and placed it in my bow. With a steady hand, I let it go. The arrow whizzed with decent speed but missed completely. I ducked by the window sill and cursed myself under my breath.

I reloaded and went back to my position. I'd aim for the closest creature. Less precision needed.

There was a creature not far from the barn door, his skin slimy and reminiscent of a slug.

I took a shot. The arrow seemed to move in slow motion as it bounced off its head. The slug-like creature turned his dead, beady eyes my way.

I slouched down under the window, but he had seen me. I grabbed another arrow and tried again. He ran toward the barn, toward me. He sure didn't move like a slug. I let the arrow go but missed again.

The slug man stopped and shook his head, unable to find the entrance. I tried again with an arrow. This time it slid deep into his side, and death was only a matter of time as he fell to the ground with an anguished scream.

Dropping down again, I hid by the window and planned my next attack. Time wasted away, and I had to make a move now. A familiar scream stopped me from reloading.

My head popped up in the window, and my eyes darted to my mom. “No. I won’t tell you.” She flailed her arms at the monster as he shook her in his hands. She was so thin and frail.

I grabbed an arrow and shot him in the back.

As he fell to the ground, his arm grabbed my mother and she fell on top of him. Her eyes filled with fright when she should have been relieved.

I didn’t have long to think as another monster walked toward her.

My father approached from behind the monster with a shovel. He swung, and the monster grabbed the shovel and forced my father back.

I had to help them. I grabbed my gear and ran from the barn toward them. I stopped within a range where I knew my shot had a chance. I readied myself and shot an arrow that narrowly missed. How could I have missed? Panic rattled me.

“Run.” My mother yelled toward me as my father waved me away. There was no way I’d have left them.

I pulled another arrow out and pushed all the negative thoughts away. I needed this one to make contact. I held myself as still as I could. Exhaling, I let another arrow fly. I managed to hit the monster in the thigh. I shot again, this time hitting him in the chest. He fell to the ground.

I ran toward the house and yelled. “Get in.”

Damour swung the door open for us, and we all collapsed on the floor as we fell in. Damour barricaded the door shut behind us.

“You shouldn’t have come here.” My mother winced as she tried to sit up.

Her voice faded into the background as the scrapes and bruises those brutes put on her became my focus.

“We need her here,” Denny, who had taken up at the window as a guard, said. “There’s too many.”

I walked over to him and peeked out. He was right. More monsters had arrived and gathered on the lawn in front of the house.

“They aren’t coming any closer,” I observed as I looked back at my family.

“Are we all here?” Vinsha’s hand shook as she placed some cups on the table.

I did a quick head count. Mother, Father, Damour, Vinsha, Denny.... Gavin?

“Gavin. Where is Gavin?” My head swung from side to side. It didn’t take long to search the small home and realize—he was out there.

"I'll go." Denny stood and grabbed the spear my father kept for protecting the farm. "Aria, back me up from the window."

"No, I'll go." I bolted toward the door, but Damour stopped me.

"Denny will go."

I couldn't respond. Shock had set in. All I could do was watch as Denny walked to the door.

Damour gave me a slight push toward the window.

I stood back as Mother kissed her son before he left to find Gavin.

"We should distract them somehow so that you can get out." The words suddenly came to me as a rush of adrenaline filled my veins.

A thunderous growl from outside rumbled our insides. Damour was the first to the window and I was second.

I skimmed the lawn, and it wasn't long until my eyes fell upon the ur'gel that had cornered me in town. With each thunderous pound of his feet, the other monsters stepped back as their leader rallied them. They huddled around him.

"What's happening?" Mother sat in her chair, weak from her injuries.

"I'm not sure." I hid a tear as I turned back to gather as much information as I could.

All we could do was watch them and try to figure out what the leader was telling them. After a few moments, they cheered and raised their weapons. Almost in a victory walk. That was when we saw why.

The lead monster walked away from his pack, toward the house, holding up Gavin by his neck. Gavin's face turned purple as his body swung back and forth in the monster's grip.

The door swung open, and Denny ran out before any of us could stop him. He yelled at the monster with the spear in his hand. The other monsters surrounded him before he could even reach their leader. They gathered around Denny and struck him over and over with their spears.

My body froze. My heart told me to run out there and fight, but my head knew it would be a death mission. There was no way I would survive. It felt wrong standing here while Denny was out there alone. My heart ached, and I realized I wasn't a good warrior.

Gavin cried out to him, but he was gone.

My mother let out a loud, agonizing scream in a voice I'd never heard before. I realized this would be one of those moments where you remembered everything. The way the sun shone through the curtains, the pattern of dust on the mantel, what your family looked like in tragedy.

Damour held onto Vinsha as she sobbed into his chest.

My father fell to his knees and stared off into the distance, quiet as a mouse. Tears teased his lashes, then fell unforgivably.

The house was silent except for the sobbing of its inhabitants. My eyes drifted from one family member to another. My heart couldn't take any more.

I gathered my strength, and my weakened body rose to the window. I needed to see Gavin, to see that he was still alive.

The monster leader stood closest to the door. He waited for us to make another mistake, to come out and fight them. He laid a frightened Gavin on the ground and surrounded him with the strongest ur'gel, somehow protecting him from us.

The leader stomped his foot on the ground, and the others stepped closer to him but kept a good foot behind him.

My stomach fluttered as my hands seemed numb.

He stopped as our eyes met through the window. Time seemed to stand still, our eyes locked, neither of us wanting to break eye contact first as if this was a game. I blinked stupidly, and he won. In that blink, he had time to throw his spear, which landed close to my head by the window frame. He could have easily made me the target.

I pushed myself to the ground and looked around the room. The others were preoccupied and missed my near-death encounter.

"Aria, stay down." Damour waved his hands toward me. "No one else dies here."

I nodded in agreement, but neither of us knew what the future held. And we were outnumbered.

"They're standing their ground." I turned toward Mother, who sat beside Vinsha. She sobbed into her hands as Vinsha rubbed her back.

I had never felt so hopeless in my life.

My father was on his knees and paid no attention to anyone. He seemed in his own world as he stared at the floor. For the first time, I saw him as older, physically and mentally not able to help us fight. It would be up to Damour and me to keep everyone safe. No, Damour had a baby on the way. I would need to be the sacrifice. If I could keep the monsters at bay, they may be able to sneak out the back.

"No." Damour's hand rubbed my arm, and it was as if he could read my mind.

I nodded for him to follow me away from everyone, and he obeyed. Out of earshot, we could discuss a plan.

"We need to get them out. And you need to live to meet your child." The muscles in my hands clenched from my nerves. I leaned over the table to flatten them out and ease the pain.

"We all get out." He nudged me away from the window to peek out. As soon, as his head popped up, an arrow slammed through the glass, and the window shattered into pieces.

"You're bleeding." I grabbed his face in my hands to examine the glass that had cut his skin.

"I'll live." He fell back against the wall. His hands shook as he placed them on his face to feel the damage.

"You have some glass embedded, but it doesn't look serious. Can you see?" I checked him over for major wounds.

"I'm fine." He turned his head in the direction of Vinsha and sent a wink her way. She missed his sweet gesture as she held the bottom of her belly and knelt on the floor.

"*Oh.*" Vinsha moaned as she sat back on the floor. "I've been having pains." She rubbed her belly. "I didn't want to say anything, but they are getting worse."

"Are you in labor?" How could this get any worse?

Another arrow shot through the door and just missed the top of Momma's head.

"Get them to the bedroom." I motioned my arms toward the room as if that would get them there quicker.

My father returned to us from whatever trance he'd been in and crawled on the floor with Mama and Vinsha to the back bedroom.

"It's her first. She needs to relax, and the cramping will go away." I grabbed my arrows and prepared for the plan we didn't have.

"You know this as a healer?"

I didn't bother to answer him. I didn't know that, but I needed him to remain calm. I kept my focus on my arrows and, out of the corner of my eye, watched as he nodded his head beside me.

"So, what do we do? They must want something." He grabbed some arrows from the floor and helped me organize them in my basket so they would be within easy reach when needed.

“I can’t think of anything of value we would have.” My thoughts clouded with images of Gavin out there alone.

I tapped Damour on the shoulder as I pointed toward the window. I lifted my head up to the side of the window to get eyes on Gavin. Instead, I almost lost my balance as the lead monster stood a few feet away from the window and locked eyes with me. I dropped to the floor. My eyes widened as I made eye contact with Damour. My finger went to my lips as I signaled for him to stay quiet. He nodded in acknowledgment.

“The boy is safe,” the monster shouted at me through the window.

My head felt light, and my shoulders tensed as the beast communicated.

“What do you want?” I cringed as I waited for more arrows to fly through the walls, but there was just silence.

“The little dreamwalker,” the monster replied.

“Dreamwalker?” Damour mouthed to me.

I let out a big sigh. There was no time to explain to Damour. This monster and Mother Ofburg had it all wrong. I wasn't a dreamwalker. I'd have known it long before now if I was.

"There is no dreamwalker here," I shouted back. Damour and I curled into little balls as we expected to be bombarded by arrows.

I caught something from the corner of my eye. I glanced back to the bedroom as our mother walked out in a stupor, her eyes glazed over, and she stood in plain sight through the window for the monster. Damour and I waved our hands frantically, telling her to get back into the bedroom. My father pulled back the curtain and crouched on the ground as he called her back.

"You are the dreamwalker they seek." The words came from my mother, but it wasn't her voice. Her arm rose as her finger pointed toward me.

"The boy will be safe," the monster spoke.

Damour lifted himself and looked out of the window.

"They are taking Gavin," Damour said.

The pit of my stomach rumbled. I stood to face the monster, to yell and scream at him for hurting my family. However, meeting him face to face silenced me.

"Bring Beru to me, and I will set this boy free." The monster turned to leave with his horde.

Smoke hung heavy around us as we burned Denny's body. We owed him a warrior's burial, but it wasn't according to ritual, considering our fear the ur'gel would return at any moment. Damour and I said our goodbyes to our brother and sent him on his next journey. We let Mother rest and Father and Vinsha stayed with her at the house. Her contractions had stopped once the monsters had left.

"He died fearlessly." Damour stood close to the fire as he made his offering. "I couldn't have done what he did."

"Me either," I admitted my fault. "But you have a child and wife. A family of your own."

We stood and gazed into the flames together, arms linked. A member of our tribe gone, lost in battle.

"It's not over. We have to get Gavin back."

"We'll find a way." Noble would know what to do. He would come into battle if I asked him. "From now on, we only plan day-to-day."

"I'll move back into the house with Vinsha."

"Vinsha and farm life?" I laughed out loud. I loved my sister-in-law, but she would not do well on a farm.

Damour smiled. It was a minute of peace in our hour of sorrow.

"She would surprise you." Damour still had a smile on his lips. It disappeared when he turned back to the fire.

"He ran this farm for Mother and Father. Are you sure you want to do that?" He had never wanted just to be a farmer. He wanted more and had found success in starting his own business.

"It's sometimes not about what you want, but what you need to do."

"I get that." No matter how many arrows had missed their target, I was a fighter.

Damour pulled up two log stumps, and we sat by the fire. I flicked a tear from my cheek. Today would be the last day I had hugged Denny.

We both stayed in silence. We wouldn't move till it burned dry. Then we would know Denny had moved on to his next life.

"I still think of him." Damour placed a gift of a flower to the fire.

"Harov?"

"They were alike, fearless." Sorrow swelled in his voice, in that he wanted to be like them. Damour had never been a fighter. He wouldn't know what to do with a spear or how to shoot an arrow.

"They're very courageous." I thought of them as little children. How stupidly fearless they were. The time they jumped from one tree to another, narrowly escaping a terrible fall.

"Sometimes dumb."

"Harov is still here."

"Is he?"

I nodded and returned my focus to the fire. Harov had chosen not to be around us. To Damour he was dead, but I understood his need to be someone else.

I didn't cry much. The last time was when Gavin had his accident. He cheated death that day, but he would never be the same. But different didn't have to mean bad. He was more cautious now and, in some ways, a better man.

A figure appeared from the direction of the house as it walked toward us.

“Is there room for one more?” Vinsha asked as she neared.

“There’s always room for you.” I smiled as I reached for her hand. She had never been through something as traumatic as the last twenty-four hours. Only new to our family for two years, she didn’t have a deep connection to our past, but we could feel her love.

“Your parents are sleeping. Mother stopped crying about an hour ago.”

My heart twinged at the thought of Mother and her pain. First her parents, who had left on a journey, never to be seen again. Then her youngest brother to illness. Now one of her sons. And Gavin? I wouldn’t let that happen.

The sight of him as he swung by the neck hadn’t left me. His eyes as they’d met mine and the fear they’d held. I’d do anything in my power to get him back.

“I think they want me.” I didn’t bother to look up for their reactions, but my head reeled as it hit me. “They followed me here.” It made sense.

"This is not your fault." Damour reached for my arm, but I leaned away from him.

"He followed me here, and I don't even know how I got here. One moment I'm in town, ready to die, then the next I'm on the farm." My eyes grew wide, and my body became enraged at the possibility I had brought this all on.

"Even if they followed you here, you didn't bring them here," Vinsha said, trying to make me feel better.

"They want me."

"Okay, so what if they do. Why?" Damour tried to play devil's advocate.

"I don't know." As the flames began to die down, so did the rage I had.

"Who is the dreamwalker that the ur'gel had spoken of?" Vinsha asked.

Damour and I glanced at each other. Neither of us wanted to explain.

Vinsha had been sheltered by her well-to-do parents. She knew nothing of the evil creatures in her own world, and my brother wanted to keep it that way.

"Dreamwalkers are able to connect with people through dreams. They can make themselves known or not." I stopped there as most of what I knew about dreamwalking wasn't very good.

"I know of one," Damour added, and his mouth frowned.

"Where?" I asked before he shut down.

"I don't know if they are still there. It's such a long time ago," Damour rebutted.

"Where?"

"He's far away. In the Western March." Damour took a deep breath.

The Western March had been a vast territory populated by the D'ahvol. They'd been outcasted by the humans and elves who had created them. With nowhere else to go, they had taken the lands that were least desirable. Low hills, rocky terrain, and wide plains. It was where plain cats, lions, forest cats, and tigers had run wild for years.

"They took him to get to me." I was desperate for them to believe me. Damour had to tell me the name of the dreamwalker he knew of. "I have to know more about dreamwalking."

"It's too dangerous." Damour turned to me and placed his hand on my knee.

"It's the only way I can get him back. I have to do this." My eyes stung with tears that had built up and begun to roll down my cheeks. It was my time to be a warrior and save Gavin.

“I can’t.” Damour turned back to the fire as his hand stroked the side of his face, conflicted and likely thinking he would be handing me a death sentence by saying anything more.

“You have to.” Vinsha leaned over to him and took his hands in hers. She was more solid than I gave her credit for.

“I’m not even sure he will talk to you about it.” Damour stood. “It’s a tricky business. He has lost family to dreamwalking.”

There would be dangers. I remembered the stories I had heard my father tell us as children. But they were fables mixed with reality, and I wasn’t sure where that line stopped.

“I can only try.” I gestured and stood beside Damour. “Please tell me what you know.”

Damour walked past me as he paced back and forth. I had decided to let him breathe before I pressured him again. After a few moments, he stopped in front of the fire, opposite us, his eyebrows low and his mouth squished up in thought.

“I’ll give you a map. I can’t take you. I need to stay here,” Damour compromised.

"I will seek a companion to join me on the journey." I hoped to convince Noble to come with me. I trusted him most and had seen him in battle. I'd be lucky to have a mentorship under him.

Damour nodded as he paced back and forth.

Vinsha offered me a weak smile. With her face pale, her body trembled even next to the fire. It appeared her contractions had started again. She smiled to herself when Damour said he would not be leaving.

"I wish you well on your journey." Vinsha stood. "I'll check on your mom and dad." She kissed Damour on the cheek and made her way back to the house.

Damour didn't return his attention to me until she entered the house. "You won't make it back. They don't take well to visitors. You won't be welcomed." Damour breathed heavily and appeared anxious as he rubbed his hands together.

"I'll be okay." I put my arms around his neck to reassure him, but his body was rigid.

"You still have much to learn," Damour whispered in my ear.

We held each other in a firm hug for several minutes, perhaps our last embrace. As Damour pulled back, a change shifted in my mind. I needed to be stronger both in a physical and mental sense. No excuses. I'd have to reign in my emotions and immaturity. My impulsive reactions needed to stop.

"You will take care of Mother and Father?" I asked of him, knowing he would. I just needed the reassurance from him. I needed him to say it.

"With my life," Damour proclaimed.

"I'll bring Gavin back," I said fiercely.

Damour shook his head in agreement but then cried. He wrapped his arms around my waist and picked me up to his full six feet stature.

"And Aria." His voice was low.

"We will both be back." I hung on to him.

He let me down, and my eyes never left him as I memorized his face in this moment.

"Be wary of anyone offering you help." Damour reached into a leather pocket that had been sewn onto his belt. He held out his closed hand and nodded for me to place my hand under it. As I did, the object fell onto my palm.

"The fool's rock." Damour pulled his arm back, revealing a shiny green stone. "Keep it on you at all times."

I smiled at the thought of his trophy coming along on this journey.

“I will.” I placed the rock in a pocket on my pants.

“I love you. And I know we don’t say such things.” Damour’s eyes darted toward the ground.

“I love you too, big brother.” I stood on my tiptoes and placed a kiss on his cheek.

I grabbed his hand and gave it a small squeeze as I headed toward the house to gather my things. I would leave that night once sleep found my family, for tonight I would embark on a warrior's journey. I only hoped it wouldn't be to the death.

I packed as little as I could for survival and avoided any more goodbyes. I had space for one more thing in my pack. I searched the little that I had and spotted a small coffee pot. Picking it up, I rubbed my hand over the dull metal. My brothers and I used to sneak cups of the strongest beans we could find when we were younger, Mother none the wiser. It could come in handy, I convinced myself, not that I could kill anyone with it if need be. But I had a feeling sleep would be limited on my journey, so the caffeine would be a necessity. I jammed it into my pack, barely able to close it.

I flung my pack over my shoulder and headed out into the dark to Mother Ofburg's to find Noble.

The woods radiated of silence and darkness, the only light coming from Gleet, our blue moon. Gleet dominated the sky, fixated on the lower, southern horizon. Comfort filled me as I reminisced about sleeping in the fields as a child with Denny and Damour. The stories we would tell Gleet.

As I got closer to Mother Ofburg's, the despair of the town increased the urgency of my pace. Many of the homes were charred, and people had huddled by fires outside. I worried about Mother Ofburg and the other healers. I had been so focused on my people I hadn't had the time to think about what could be going on here.

The gates to the property were demolished, broken to pieces. My stomach dropped at the sight of the healing hut and outbuildings. Two burned to the ground, and anything left standing badly damaged. As I approached the main house where Mother Ofburg lived, a glimmer of light shined through the window, the glass no longer intact.

I moved toward it, wanting to delay any pain that could come as I entered the hut. I had to step over a body that hadn't been taken away yet. Something that would have been done if everything were fine.

I gathered myself as I walked to the door. Things would not be the same when I passed the threshold. I placed my hand on the doorknob and tried to turn it, but it stuck. I pulled and tugged as hard as I could.

"Who's there?" I could hear Mother Ofburg's voice from inside.

"It's me." I pulled on the doorknob harder. Finally, I let go, and the door fell to my side.

“Aria.” Mother Ofburg was quickly by my side and wrapped me in her arms. “We thought the worst when we couldn’t find you.” She pulled back from me as her eyes searched my person for any injuries.

“I’m fine. I went home to check on my parents.”

She pulled me by my arm into the room and lifted up a chair that was on its side for me to sit down in.

“Did they make it through?” Mother Ofburg poured me a glass of her best whiskey, which was almost gone.

“Denny’s gone.” I choked back the need to vomit, having said it out loud for the first time.

“My condolences to your family.” Mother Ofburg leaned in closer to me as she handed me my glass of whiskey and motioned for me to drink from it.

I obliged.

“He died trying to save Gavin. The ur'gel took him with them when they left.” I let out a large exhausted breath.

“They took Gavin?” Mother Ofburg sat back in her chair and shook her head.

“I’m going to get him back. I need Noble to come to Western March with me. There’s a dreamwalker there that will help me find Gavin." I somehow needed her permission to take this journey.

"No." Mother Ofburg abruptly stood and walked away from me, shaking her hands.

"What do you mean no?" I followed her to the next room.

"The dreamwalker." She stopped and turned her head back at me.

"I can't help what I am."

"You're the reason they're all dead." Mother Ofburg's voice grew loud as her arms waved around.

"Who is dead?" I wondered who she was specifically talking about.

"Noble. Noble is dead." Mother Ofburg's eyes spat at me.

"What are you talking about?"

"Get out of my house," Mother Ofburg screamed at me as she punched me hard. Something seemed to possess her.

"He's not dead." My gut heaved at the thought of never seeing Noble again.

"Get out. Destruction will follow you," Mother Ofburg yelled over and over as I fled.

I burst out of the doorway and ran outside to hide. Another person I loved dearly taken from me.

"Noble!" I yelled into the wind as I hoped Mother Ofburg was wrong.

I laid on the cold ground and lost track of time. My will had been taken away, and I drowned myself in my losses. My heart ached, and breath was elusive.

I awoke hours later. At first, I ignored the need to get up, for having the bliss of sleep meant I didn't have to remember what had happened.

My eyelids burned, and my body pained. I opened my eyes and noticed two feet standing in front of me. I flipped over on my back and grabbed the first thing in reach to protect myself—a stalk of corn.

"Now what are you going to do with that?" Marina chuckled.

Marina, a new healer, sat on a stack of hay as she watched me. She was childlike but took to healing like I never had.

"Sorry, I must still be in fight mode." I got up on my feet.

“I overheard you and Mother Ofburg yesterday. I’m sorry you had to find out about Noble that way.” Marina’s eyes drifted from me.

I didn’t want her talking about him, so I didn’t bother to reply. Instead, I just nodded.

“He died quickly, in case you wanted....” Marina’s voice trailed off.

Again, I nodded to her.

“He wanted me to tell you that he loved you and that you should do whatever it is that you’re always telling him you wanted to do. He didn’t tell me what that was,” Marina added.

“Thank you for telling me.” I hung my head low. I didn’t want to cry in front of her.

“I also want to help.” Marina smiled at me and stepped closer. “Sade Lemm is getting ready to leave. She’s headed into the Northern Territory. She picked up some supplies from Mother Ofburg. You might be able to tag along,” Marina finished in a whisper.

“Did she mention why she was headed there?”

“No. I should go. Mother Ofburg wanted me to help some of the children find food for their families.”

Marina stepped backward for a few feet then turned and ran to the front of the hut. "She's in the cave, but I'm not sure for how long." Marina disappeared into the hut.

I didn't waste any time. I grabbed what I came with and headed to the caves. It would take me some time to discover what one she was in, though. I entered each cave, not knowing what creature could be hiding in them. The first two held displaced townspeople. They hadn't even known Sade had been amongst them.

I chose a cave off to the side next. It would have been the one I would have used if I had wanted to be alone.

"Sade?" My voice echoed in the cavities.

Silence.

I turned to leave, but something caught my eye. I turned back, and before me stood the most beautiful white wolf. I froze at the thought of it ripping me apart in mere seconds.

"Easy." I stepped back and off to the side in case it wanted to get out of the cave.

One small movement and I slipped, falling to the ground.

The wolf came closer and bared its sharp teeth.

I backed away from it from the ground as I crawled backward out of the cave.

It jumped with a loud growl, and I froze in fear. It leaned back on its hind legs as if it would pounce on me. My arm flew over my eyes to protect myself.

I sat in darkness as nothing happened.

“Kid. Pass me my clothes. Over there.”

I moved my arm from my eyes. Sade stood naked in front of me, comfortable in her skin.

I followed her arm to a pile of clothes on the ground and retrieved them for her. How could I forget she was part wolf?

I sat back against the wall and averted my eyes while she dressed.

“I’m sorry about Noble.” She pulled on her shirt. “He was a good man.”

“He was.” I nodded, and for a moment I was jealous, wondering if anything had happened between them besides fighting in battle together. “Denny passed.”

“My condolences. I hadn’t heard.” Her movement was slow as if she was deep in thought.

“Thank you.”

“This battle brought much loss.” Sade packed up her scattered belongings in the cave, most covered in blood.

“Too much.”

“Died trying to save you?”

“Yes, and my family.”

Sade nodded.

“So why are you here, kid? Poking around these mountains is not very smart given the past few days.”

“I heard you were going to the Northern Territory.”

“I don’t need a healer.”

Sade averted her attention back to her pack again, lifting it onto her shoulders.

“I’m not a healer, really,” I bantered back, getting to my feet, prepared to follow her if she did not take me with her.

“No. No, you’re not.” Sade stood back with her weight on one leg and stared straight through me. “You’re not ready, though.”

Sade picked up her walking stick and left the cave.

"I have a good reason to come along," I called after her, barely keeping up.

"No," she called back to me over her shoulder.

"But you don't even know the reason."

"You seek revenge." She stopped, and I walked into her—hard. Hard enough to fall back on the ground and embarrass myself.

"Just hear me out." I tried to sound as reasonable as I could from the ground.

"Fine." Sade plopped herself on the ground next to me. "Go."

My head jumbled, and I didn't know what to say. She was so strong and fearless. Everything I aspired to be.

"This is going to sound a little crazy," I braced her. "I feel it a calling, to fight those who attacked us."

"You would die in five minutes." She cut me off but stayed in her spot. I had her interest.

"Okay, I need to see a dreamwalker there." I paused, knowing she would interrupt me again.

"Go on, kid." Sade leaned in.

"I think the ur'gel were here for me." I paused again, but she remained quiet. I couldn't gauge her expression. "Because I can dreamwalk."

"That could be useful. You're certain they came for you?"

"Yes," I responded.

"Makes sense. They never come on that hard and strong." Sade wrapped her arms around her legs and rocked back and forth, still with her gaze on me.

"They'll keep attacking, if I don't see the dreamwalker."

"What you got in the bag?" She nodded toward my bag, a fourth the size of hers. "Any food?"

"Rice." I swung it toward her for inspection.

She loosened the top of the bag and emptied it onto the ground, rifling through it.

"A coffee pot?" she said, clearly confused as she picked it up. "It's half the size of this bag." She flung it back over her head into the woods and continued her inspection through the rest of my items.

"Wait!" I tried to catch it in midair and failed miserably.

Sade threw my pack back at me with the items she deemed usable.

"So, can I come?"

"How do you know that you can dreamwalk?" Sade went back into a rocking position.

"Because I did it one night." I rubbed the scar that was starting to form on my hand.

"So, you mean, you could have been dreamwalking most of your life and not known it?" Sade appeared amused.

"That's possible." I tied the top of my pack together in case she decided to take off again.

"Why do you need to see another dreamwalker?"

"They took my brother, Gavin." I hadn't wanted to tell her that just yet.

Sade rocked back and forth in the grass, staring at me with an uncaring look on her face.

I figured I could either follow her or find someone else to take me. The only other person I could think of would be Skyra, but the Council Three would never let her.

"Fine. You can come. But you better not slow me down, and if you get in trouble for being stupid, I'll leave you." Sade got up on her feet and started down a path.

I scrambled to my feet and followed her. I hoped could trust her to take me to the Western March.

We walked for most of the morning without speaking, mainly due to me trying to catch my breath and keep up with Sade. She was used to covering a lot of ground in little time, and she wasn't waiting for me. Her long legs stretched out with each stride while my shorter legs needed to jog.

"We'll rest here." Sade stopped.

I nodded, thankful for the break. I dropped my small pack on the ground and then lay down on the grass. I spread myself out like an eagle, thankful for the cold ground to relax.

"Is that a healer thing, kid?" Sade stood over me, looking down at me like I was a foreign animal.

"It's a relaxing thing. You should try it." I rolled over on my belly and leaned on my elbows.

"Not likely." Sade dug through her backpack.

I admired her for her lack of caring. She said what she meant and didn't dance around it.

"Here." Sade threw a bag of corn toward me. "Cook."

I bit my tongue against a comeback and grabbed the corn. I got up to gather some wood for the fire as Sade took care of the pot and firepit. I lugged a few medium pieces of wood back to burn.

"Your brother, Gavin, he can't walk." Sade stepped back as I took over the cooking.

"He had an injury at a young age," I replied, unsure of how much she knew. It had been quite a scandal as my parents were blamed for Gavin's unruly ways.

"Magic. Wasn't it?"

"Something like that." I remained quiet and hoped she would take the hint. I focused on building a fire and making the corn she wanted.

"He had been off by one ingredient." Sade's eyes never left me.

"What?"

"He used black wolf urine instead of white." Sade crossed her legs and sat closer to the fire.

"How do you know?"

"He came to me just before." Sade added more wood to my fire.

"And you wouldn't help him?" I glared at her.

"No. With his spell, it wouldn't have worked." Sade lay back on the grass. She stretched out her arms and legs and let out a deep sigh. "You're right, this is relaxing."

"Why didn't you tell him it wouldn't work?" I stood, half not believing this conversation.

"He wouldn't listen. Runs in your family." Sade sat up.

"You didn't give him your urine."

"If he'd had my urine, he would have died." Sade plopped back on the grass and let out another deep sigh. "You're welcome."

I took my place by the campfire again, not bothering to say another word. She could dump me at any point, and what had happened then wouldn't change the path I was on today. I focused on cooking the corn and biting my tongue.

I grabbed the plate Sade had brought with her and dropped her corn on it. "It's done." I placed it on the ground.

"You're not having any?" Sade took her plate.

"I'm not hungry." I focused on the fire. The dancing flames always called me. The peace of a fire revived my soul.

"You would keep up better if you ate." Sade dug into her food without a care it hadn't had time to cool.

I still longed to be like her, but there was a big difference between us. Perhaps she could be a great warrior because she didn't care as much. Perhaps that part of her turned off when her parents died.

"Okay. Ask me anything you want." Sade ate the last of her corn. "Let's get this over with. Then maybe all this talking could stop."

"How do you do it?" I asked, not quite sure of the right words to use.

"Kill?"

"Be a warrior. A good warrior." I waited for her to release all her secrets

"You don't want to be like me."

"I need to fight better. I've practiced, but I need the strategy part. Will you teach me?" I leaned in as I hoped any part of my story would appeal to her.

Sade stood quiet and, like always, was hard to get a read on.

"This is your journey. You'll get out of it what you want. I have no say in that." Sade threw some gravel on our campfire to put it out. "You should have eaten."

She was right. It was my journey. I was a fighter, just not a particularly good one—yet. Being a warrior wasn't meant to be fun or cool. That was the opposite of what it meant.

I dug in my backpack and took out an apple to eat. Sade used some hay growing in the field and scrubbed her pot clean. No one spoke until every task was completed.

"It's time to go." Sade walked back to the path we had come off before our break.

I rushed to grab my things and followed her.

"So, this ur'gel thing. They are following you?" Sade slowed her pace so I could keep up.

"It's the only thing that makes sense."

"And the D'ahvol. Do you know much about them?"

I bit my lip. I should know more. "I only know the rumors," I uttered and waited for her to scold me.

"There are a few cities there. Most are controlled by the D'ahvol, who as you should know, are half-human and half-elf. They are quite large and intelligent. It will be a different fight than the ur'gel."

"And they have no magic abilities?"

"If they aren't a mixed breed, no. But those creatures don't tend to stay home." Sade stopped as we came to a fork in the road. "Which way?"

"What do you mean? You don't know how to get there?"

"Do you want me to teach you or not?" Sade hung her head back and sighed. "Look for the signs. Which way should we go?"

I walked closer to each path, unsure of what I should be looking for. I tried to notice the differences between the paths.

"This one." I pointed to the path on the left.

"Why?" Sade stepped to the left of me.

"It's broken down more. You mentioned they were large."

"Let's go." Sade took off on the left path.

I guessed I had passed her test.

"I picked the right one?"

"We won't know till we get there."

"So, you don't know where we are going?"

"It's west. It works," Sade said.

We walked for a few miles without talking. I took note. The less we spoke, the slower she walked, so I took my hint.

We came upon a spring, and Sade took off her pack. It was time for another break.

"It's quite breathtaking," I said as I took in the waterfall.

"We don't need small talk, kid. Just enjoy it."

I wet myself down with the cool water to be refreshed.

"I'm ready to fight too," I broke the silence. This far in, she wouldn't leave me if I annoyed her.

"And to die?"

"If it comes to that."

Sade scooped up a large handful of water and splashed her face. "It will."

"Then mentor me." I left my perch and walked toward her. I squatted down a few feet from her.

"You're taking on too much too fast." Sade continued to cool down in the water.

"I have no choice. I need a backup plan if the ur'gel deceive me."

"The ur'gel are not the best way to do this." Sade took a seat on a rock in the shade.

"What do you mean?"

"To get your brother back. Fighting the ur'gel didn't work last time. I wouldn't trust them enough to dreamwalk for them either. Those are your only two options." Sade picked up a pear that had fallen off a tree.

"You mean they could be tricking me?"

"Or worse." Sade looked off into the distance. Her eyebrows lowered.

"What?"

"Shhh...." Sade waved her arm at me to sit down. She made her way over to me and pointed to the path we had just left. "I think I heard something."

We both stayed in silence and watched for any movement in the trees. After a while, Sade stood.

"I think we're okay, but let's not stick to a path. We aren't in town anymore." Sade went back and took another pear.

I stayed on the ground, a little more cautious, and kept my eyes on the path just in case.

"You need to get Gavin without fighting the ur'gel."

"How do I do that?" My eyes went between her and the path.

"Figure it out." Sade grabbed a third pear. She gathered another and threw it at me to eat.

I missed the catch and received an eye roll from Sade.

"I barter with dreamwalking. I could make up something to hold them off until I have Gavin."

"That's a crappy plan, but at least you're thinking." Sade scooped some water up in her hands to drink.

While her words may not be "emotional," her heart was in the right place. In her own way, she was helping me become a great fighter.

"You need more passion," Sade offered with the least bit of passion in her voice.

"Passion?" I was confused at her thought process.

"Without passion, you will never be a great warrior. What's your reasoning for being a fighter?"

I sat back and thought for a moment. I guess I didn't have one except for wanting to be one. "To be looked up to."

"Vanity. Try again." Sade's voice was jagged. "You need something more. What's fighting mean to you?"

"It would mean I'm confident, that I could protect people."

"Wrong." Sade sighed. "Again." She waved her hand in the air.

"That I'm worth something," I replied, unsure if I had said it out loud.

Sade was quiet. No quick comments back. "Okay, listen. We will go to see this dreamwalker and get your questions answered. I'll take you to Western March." Sade took off to the left of path into the woods, back to the fork in the road.

"We were going the wrong way? Why didn't you say anything?"

"I want to help you now," Sade yelled back to me.

I forced myself to remain calm. I needed Sade to take me to the dreamwalker, so I could learn how to dreamwalk properly. Somehow the man in my dreams was connected to all of this, but I couldn't figure out how.

He was there, a few feet in front of me, alone while he cooked a rat carcass over the fire. A tattered white bandage was wrapped around his hand where he had been injured the last time I saw him. The first time I knew I had dreamwalked. I approached, but he didn't glance my way.

"Hello," I called toward him.

He never flinched. It was as if he couldn't see or hear me.

I walked toward his camp. I could hear him whispering to himself, some sort of chant or prayer, but couldn't make out the words. I paused a few feet away from him and thought of how I could reach him. There was a seat on the opposite side of the fire from him, so I used it as my perch.

The man's gaze slipped from the fire as he methodically surveyed his surroundings. Then he sniffed the air. Perhaps he *could* sense me.

I leaned in closer as his attention returned to his meal, yet his eyes remained on guard, twitching from side to side.

"Can you hear me?" I said, my voice a little choppy. I half hoped he couldn't.

He didn't move.

I had to get through to him. I didn't know when I would see him again. I glanced around as I searched for something I could use to communicate with him. I leaned down to pick up a stick with the intention of throwing it in the fire. I decided against that. If he couldn't see or hear me, that would just frighten him. I'd use that as a last resort.

Then it came to me. I'd use healing. I closed my eyes and tried to garner enough energy to make myself visible to him. I stood and placed my hands out in front of me as I tried to holster energy from around me. My fingers trembled as energy filled my body.

Just as soon as I gathered the energy, I abruptly lost it, almost toppling over from dizziness. Why didn't I listen to those magic teachings? I glanced back at the man, now eating his carefully charred rat. My hand flew to my mouth at the crunching sounds, which made me ill.

I took my place back on the log and tried to think of something I could use to communicate with him.

I noticed a patch of sand and hoped he could read. I grabbed a stick and wrote a message. The man jumped back from his log and grunted as his head swung from side to side. I needed to write the message faster.

I've been called to help you.

The man yelled in another language I could not understand. He shielded himself with his arm over his face, then he came forth to read my message.

I tried again to harness energy from Lynia, to show myself to him, and after a few minutes of deep concentration and the help of the fool's rock my brother had given me, I began to appear in form.

"Witch!" the man yelled at me as he grabbed his knife and held it up. He lunged, but I was quicker.

"I'm a healer."

His eyes were wild and darted back and forth.

I held my hands out to him to show I was no threat.

"I'm here to help you."

"Where have you come from?" The man held up his knife in my direction.

What would happen, if he killed me while dreamwalking?

"I'm from Low Forest. I'm a healer, and I have been sent here to help you," I said very fast as I tried to see any signs of reasoning on his face.

"By whom?" He moved to the left.

I quickly countered, ensuring the same distance remained between us.

"The ur'gel." I hoped this dance would end and we could talk. I didn't have much time left.

He appeared to be calmer, his body less tense. "You can't free me. You're on a suicide mission."

My eyes wandered back to him as he sat back down on his log to eat. The knife remained within hand's reach.

"How long have you been here?" I sat across from him again.

"Two hundred and fifty years. Abouts." He spit bone out of the side of his mouth.

I remembered my father telling me stories about the Dark War. This man had been in jail since then?

"What's your name?" I needed to know more about the man I was supposed to save.

He sat back, and his eyes roamed my body,

I became increasingly aware of my surroundings and had to force my leg from bouncing. I was still as I could be as I waited to see if he would respond.

"Yours first." He stuck another dead rat on the end of his stick and hung it out over the fire.

"Aria Trevil," I said, wary of his next move.

"Trevil." He glanced up from his cooking and nodded his head in respect.

When I didn't react, he hung his head low. "You don't even know of your people."

"What do you mean?"

"The Trevils were good fighters. Trustworthy." His body relaxed a little bit.

"And your name?" I hoped he would offer it up this time.

"Beru Halsted."

I sucked in a breath at the mention of Beru. The ur'gel had burned this name within my very soul.

"I'm here to get you out of this place. I don't have a plan yet, but I will."

"I've been here for two-hundred-and-fifty-years, little girl. Don't you think if there were a way to escape, I'd have found it?"

"I'll find a way." I wasn't about to let this monster ruin my plans to save my brother. He would get on board.

"What are you doing working for the ur'gel?" He sat back.

"You're not a very gracious host," I blurted out, feeling uncomfortable in his company. I didn't know who he was or what he had done to be stuck here.

"They are making you do this." He sat back and laughed. "Of all the people to send. A little girl.

"I will save you from here, not because you don't deserve to spend the rest of your life in here but because I'm a professional." I stood and tried to remain calm, but he rattled my nerves.

Beru raised and threw off his wolf fur. His muscles gleamed as the moon hit them. With one leap, he jumped over the fire, and he was mere inches from me. His head a good two feet above mine as he stared down at me, into my soul. I closed my eyes for fear he could hear my thoughts, then his hand cupped my chin and lifted it. He leaned in and whispered in my ear, "Don't worry. I'd never hurt a child."

"Be quiet." A hand shook me as I opened my eyes, and Sade knelt over me.

“Where am I?” I sat up and looked around for Beru.

“In the woods, where else would you be?” Sade sat back down beside me. “Practically yelling for the ur’gel to come and get us.”

“The ur’gel?”

“I’ve been scouting them since you fell asleep. They marched north early this morning down the path.” Sade didn’t hide her annoyance with me.

“I’m sorry, I was dreamwalking. Not quite sure how.” I wrapped my arms around my knees. Beru’s musk still strong in my nostrils.

“If you end up in a coma, I’ll leave you here.” Sade rolled up her blanket and that was my cue to pack up camp.

“I know.” I rolled my eyes and flopped back on the bed I had made from grass last night. I closed my eyes and sank into a daydream of his hand touching my face. There was something so familiar about him.

“Don’t move.” Sade hung low to the ground and looked down the hill.

I turned my head, unable to see anything, but I heard them.

“Biggest group yet, about fifty to sixty,” Sade whispered.

We stayed still for quite some time until they all passed. It gave me time to memorize my encounter with Beru. Was he still thinking about me? What was he doing? I was addicted to wanting to know him more.

“I think that’s it.” Sade stood and stretched her neck out in the direction of the trails.

“What do you think they are doing?”

“Going home. They live in the desert next to the Western March.” Sade knelt to finish packing up. “Are you just going to sleep while I do all the work?”

I took her hint and got up to disassemble the homemade bedding we prepared the night before. It was important not to leave any indications we had been here.

“Did you see him again?” Sade asked from behind me.

“I did,” I replied, still uncertain as to how much I wanted to tell her.

“And?”

“At first he couldn’t see me.” I took the last bit of grass and threw it in the woods. “But I figured out how to communicate with him.

“Can he help get Gavin back?”

“He’s been in prison for two hundred and fifty years.” I half laughed.

“Since the Dark War.” Her tone was serious.

My smile left my face as I figured it wasn’t something to laugh about.

“I didn’t expect that.”

“Me either.”

“Does he look two-hundred-and-fifty-years-old?” Sade poked at me and surprised me with a grin.

“No. He’s rugged.”

“Do I detect a crush?” Sade raised one eyebrow.

“Of course not.” The thought of him and I made me gag. Sure, he was okay on the eyes, but any good qualities were lost to his know-it-all attitude.

“So, you have thought about it.” Sade nudged my arm.

“No.” I turned my head to hide my red cheeks from her.

“So, what else happened? Come on, amuse me.” Sade finished the last bit of camp break down.

“This isn’t for your amusement.” I walked over to a fruit tree and filled my bag. If only I could take these to Beru.

"We have miles to cover, kid. We have to have some fun." Sade tossed an apple at my pack with a chuckle.

"He was eating rat." I put one more fruit in my bag.

"Yummy." Sade smiled over her shoulder.

"He murmured something under his breath, but I couldn't make it out. It wasn't in our language." I hoped she would have some insight.

"Well, he roamed the earth long ago. Do you remember any words?"

"No. Even if I did, I would be able to pronounce it."

Sade didn't turn her head back this time to reply. Instead, she walked along the path a little faster.

"He kept saying it over and over, almost like a prayer just before he ate," I said a little louder.

"Many people pray...." Sade's voice drifted off.

"Yes. His body language was different, and his mood—"

"I hope we don't see any more ur'gel," Sade cut me off. It was a legit concern, but it seemed to be the wrong timing.

"Is something wrong?"

Sade stopped and turned toward me. “No, why would there be?”

I nodded and walked beside her.

“Oh, he told me his name,” I said

Sade didn’t reply and maintained one step in front of me.

“Did you hear me?” I pulled at her arm to stop.

“Yes, I’m not deaf,” Sade replied.

“Do you want to know it?” I asked, confused at how this conversation was going. Only a few moments ago, she had wanted to know everything.

Sade shrugged.

“Beru Halsted.” I half expected her to tell me all about him. Well, I had hoped she would.

“That’s a horrible name for a prisoner.” Sade turned and kept walking, faster.

Had I just seen that correctly? Did Sade’s eyes appear to be watering?

“Do you know him?” I jogged a few steps to catch up with her.

“Do I look ancient?” she called back over her shoulder, managing to still walk faster than my jog. Something was off.

"We need to make it another few miles, then we'll camp in the caves. It's going to rain tonight," Sade said.

My eyes drifted toward the sky. It was clear and light blue, no clouds in sight.

Sade stopped responding and picked up her speed. I tried to keep up as best as I could, but with the ur'gel around, there was no way to continue with our conversation. We marched on and kept on guard as we advanced through the woods.

After what seemed like significant progress, Sade veered off course, and we found a spot to take a break, much to my liking. We stopped by a stream to get cleaned up and drank as much as we could.

"I needed this break." I tried my best to relax before Sade wanted to get back into the woods.

Sade headed over to the stream, and at first, I thought she hadn't heard me, but the twisted look of her lips told me she had.

"It's not much longer." Sade soaked her socks in the water and rang them out. "Think you can get back by yourself?"

Her comment stunned me. I hadn't thought about getting back home. I had assumed she would be heading home after our little trip.

"Yes." I wanted to sound certain and confident, but I was anything but. I didn't have any adventure training. We had always relied on Skyra or someone else from Council Three.

"I'm not sure about what your plan is." Sade had seemed distant ever since I had told her about my dream, and it was getting on my last nerve to know why already.

"My only plan is to rescue Gavin." I tried to keep my composure.

"He may be dead already. I know you don't want to hear that, but I think you should be ready."

"I'm ready for anything." I shook my shirt hard and took her comment out on it.

"I don't see this ending well." Sade put her socks and shoes back on.

"Thanks," I muttered with my head down. I would rather she be quiet than to talk like this.

"May not seem like it, but I'm just looking out for you," Sade said. "This kind of magic isn't one I would even mess with."

"If you had a family, you would understand." The words tumbled out, and I regretted them as soon as my lips closed. "I'm sorry. I'm upset and didn't mean to say that to you." I wouldn't blame Sade if she left me where I lay.

Sade didn't bother to say anything back to me. Why did I have to be such a jerk sometimes? She took off to the trail, and I made sure to follow her so she couldn't lose me.

Again, we walked in silence, but this time, Sade kicked her feet on the ground and made more noise than before. Her recklessness made me nervous as the ur'gel had marched this way.

"Shouldn't we be quieter?" I looked around us.

"You already have a death wish, may as well get it over with," Sade replied.

I yanked on her arm to get her to turn back to me.

"Don't you think this is childish? Okay, I said something stupid. I'm sorry. I swear it will never happen again."

Sade grabbed me by my shoulders and pushed me back into the brush. She fell on top of me. About to fight her off, she placed her hand over my mouth and put her finger to her lips, her eyes wide. At first their voices were faint. Then they became louder as the ur'gel marched toward us.

They passed on the path we just walked on. A slight movement and they would see us. I closed my eyes and laid my head back. We waited as a hundred of them passed by us. As their footsteps grew softer, Sade fell off me to my side.

"Ok. I think we are good." Sade spit dirt out from her mouth.

"That's too close." I sat up and stretched my back.

"A little too close." Sade got up and peeked out on the path. "We could continue, but it'll be difficult with them in front of us. If we stick to the woods, we'll make more noise."

The sound of thunder rumbled in the distance, and sprinkles of rain began to fall.

"There's no caves near, and it's too dangerous to camp on the paths." Sade craned her neck and looked in each direction.

"What do we do?" The rain fell harder and soaked my clothes.

"Follow me." Sade ran.

I tried my best to keep up with her, even though she'd taken me on the path ur'gel were just seen on.

"There is a path just up here that brings us to an abandoned shed."

We kept as quiet as we could, thankful for the rain covering any noise we made. Then the rain lessened.

We could smell fire, so we drifted off the path and made our way closer to the smell by the woods. We came upon the ur'gel campsite. We hid behind some shrubs and studied the layout of their camp. Where they slept, ate, and played.

"They are the ones from town, that attacked us." I recognized a few of the monsters.

"It doesn't look like they did any raiding."

We watched as they milled about their camp until dusk set. Sade pulled me back and pointed toward the back of the camp. It was Gavin, chained to a chair.

Sade's hand covered my mouth. "Don't say anything stupid."

I nodded my head, yes, and she removed her hand.

"He's alive," I whispered to myself because I hadn't believed he would be. I was certain once they had left that they would have murdered him.

"He's surrounded by about two hundred ur'gel." Sade's tone of voice brought me back to reality. Even though he was right in front of my eyes, I still couldn't save him.

We both sat down in the shrubs in silence.

"I'm going to save him."

"How did I know you were going to say that?" Sade cracked her neck.

"I won't have to save Beru if I can get Gavin tonight." I grabbed Sade's arm, but she brushed me off.

"And you will have some fast monsters after you as soon as you step out. You'll both be dead."

I had noticed she hadn't included herself in that analogy.

"Will you help me?" I held my breath.

"No. It's a bad idea. I'm not down for this." Sade reached into her backpack and pulled out a knife and handed it to me. "The tip is poisoned for one cut."

"You're leaving?" I felt queasy at the thought of carrying on this journey alone. My hand reached out to grab her arm. I regretted it as she turned to me and plucked my hand right off her.

"I told you that if you're going to make a stupid choice, I'm not going to stick around." Sade turned back to finish gathering her things.

I sat back on the ground and wrapped my arms around my waist, rocking back on my heels. I had to decide if I was going to carry on with Sade and save Gavin later, or take my chance now and try to remember how to get back with Gavin, who couldn't walk. The choice seemed obvious. However, I couldn't leave Gavin behind.

Sade looked back at me one last time. "So, what's it going to be? Continue or die?"

I could appreciate Sade's humor, but I had a hard time believing if Sade were in my shoes, she would just walk away.

"I'm going to get my brother," I said without hesitation. My heart couldn't leave him there. He needed me.

Sade stood there and looked toward the ground.

I hoped she felt conflicted and would stay, but I couldn't ask her to do that. She was right. I very well could be walking into a death trap.

"Wait till it's at its darkest. They will be drunk and slower. Enter from behind. You have one chance to do this." Sade picked up the last of her things and turned to head out.

I watched as she walked away and hoped she would turn back and say, "Got ya!" and stay with me. Soon, however, I was alone. I had to dig deep, but all my insecurities shone. My feet froze to the ground, and I had little energy to move.

I still had time to tame these butterflies. I would wait till complete darkness, and enter their camp and take Gavin.

After a few moments, the queasy feeling left me as I was ready to deal with the task at hand. I crawled on my knees to a better vantage point. I found the best spot to keep track of Gavin and planted myself in the woods. I barely took my eyes off him.

The same ur'gel guarded him. They mustn't have thought of him to be much of a threat as he couldn't walk, which I'd use to my advantage. As I sat there and scoped out Gavin's location, I felt more at ease. My energy was in the right place, and I was ready to fight if I had to.

With fewer ur'gel around him, I might be able to do this. My hand drifted to the sheath the knife Sade gave me was in. One ur'gel, one poisoned tip.

Deep in thought, I almost hadn't noticed when the ur'gel that guarded Gavin left him and walked toward the party. No one came to replace him. I sprinted as fast as I could to get to Gavin.

"Aria. What are you doing here?" Gavin said through gritted teeth.

"I'm getting you out of here." I tried to loosen his hands from the rope the ur'gel had tied him to a tree with. The knot was very tight, and for a moment, my head began to spin and my hands shook. I lost all confidence.

"Pull on the top," Gavin instructed.

I did as he said as my mind went blank, and the knot loosened.

"How did you know?" I worked on the ropes.

"I've had some time to think about getting out of here," he said sarcastically. "I may not be able to walk, but I'm not an invalid."

I ignored his sass, and I focused on freeing him.

"How did you find me?" Gavin kept guard on the group of partying ur'gel.

"Sade Lemm. We were on our way to Western March, and we came upon the camp." I tried to keep my concentration on the task at hand instead of on the large group of ur'gel a few feet away.

"Sade Lemm helped you?" Gavin appeared shocked Sade would help. Any reasonable person would be. I wanted to ask about the extent of Gavin and Sade's relationship. He had gone to her when he needed help, which made me mad he didn't come to me.

"That doesn't matter now." I pulled on the last part of the knot, and Gavin was freed. I let out a quick sigh then tried to lift him, but he was weak and dead weight.

"Have they been feeding you?" His arms had already lost some muscle weight, and my hands rubbed against his ribs as I lifted him.

"They weren't very interested in my needs." Gavin clasped his hands together around my neck.

"I'll fix that as soon as we are safe." I glanced back at the ur'gel that had been guarding Gavin. He was getting rather drunk and had no interest in his guard duty.

"He won't be back for a while. Sometimes he forgets about me till morning."

"Did they tell you why they took you?" The loudness of the party rattled me. It would be hard to hear if anyone approached. They organized battles between each other. Many were bloodied, but all were laughing.

"They don't seem the sharing type." Gavin pointed to a black blanket. "Grab that. I'll drape it over my back so they don't see us."

I did as he said and took note of other provisions the ur'gel had in their camp. I grabbed food, fire starters, and a coffee pot. For a brief moment, my mind shifted to the coffee pot Sade threw away. I grabbed a pack by Gavin's bed and stuffed everything in it, including the coffee pot.

"Can you hold this while on my back?" I handed him the bag to test the weight.

"I'll try my best." He nodded, and we got to work.

I balanced Gavin on my back as I leaned forward and hung on to his arms that were wrapped around my neck. We had about twenty feet to the forest. Once there, I would run as fast I could for as long as I could. Maybe we could catch up to Sade if she had headed back. I used that thought as my motivation to move faster.

"Hurry," Gavin whispered in my ear. He hung on to the bag just fine, but I immediately regretted the coffee pot, not thinking the bag could be dropped. I grabbed a piece of the bag with my teeth for added measure.

He was much heavier than I had anticipated, and his lack of control in his legs made his balance difficult to regulate. He was also taller than I, so I had to contend with his feet as they dragged on the ground. The only other option was to take the chair the ur'gel had fashioned for him and wheel him out, but that would be slow and noisy.

I did my best as I dragged him. I focused on one spot in the woods and moved as fast as I was able to. We were going to make it. Phase one almost complete.

"Almost there. You're doing it," Gavin said in my ear as he encouraged me.

A rope lassoed us and pulled us backward. We fell on the grass and Gavin yelled in pain. I rolled over and yanked on the rope to loosen it as the ur'gel who had attacked our house and taken Gavin stood over us with a scowl on his face.

The ur'gel had his followers restrain Gavin and me. They took us to what appeared to be the main tent. They bound our hands behind our backs and pushed me into a sitting position. They brought Gavin's chair in for him to sit.

We sat in front of a fire and waited. I glanced toward Gavin, and one of the ur'gel stepped forward. I turned back to the fire.

The main ur'gel entered the tent and took his place in an ornate wooden chair with intricate carvings on the arms and legs. It was covered in plush leather. However, I did not recognize the animal. It must have been rare. This ur'gel must have been someone important in his community.

"The dreamwalker and the invalid." The ur'gel spoke as a woman, a human, served him a drink.

I bit my tongue since we were outnumbered. I was in his house.

"You don't speak?" He directed his comment to me as he waved his followers away.

The ur'gel approached us, and to my surprise, they unbound our hands. One of the ur'gel brought over a chair for me to sit at next to the table.

"My apologies for the rough treatment. You caused quite a stir with your arrival." The ur'gel stated as his human remained by his side, ready to serve him.

"Do you know my brother has barely eaten since you captured him?" I stared at the ur'gel as it was the only thing I could do at the moment without getting us killed.

"No, I did not know this." The ur'gel turned his head toward his followers. "Is this true?"

The ur'gel lowered their heads and didn't meet his scrutiny.

"Then you must bring him food now, and our guest." The ur'gel nodded, and his two followers scurried out of the tent. "My apologies. They are sometimes thick in the head. I assure you that a starved prisoner is not my intent."

"Thank you." I sat back in the chair a little looser now. I didn't trust the ur'gel. However, he was much calmer and agreeable than in past meetings.

"I admire you, Aria, if I may call you that."

I nodded yes.

"You may call me Xagu."

He smiled and clapped his hands, as his followers returned with a feast of food and drink. The food was placed on a table, and once it was arranged, Xagu joined us. I stood to wheel Gavin over, but Xagu lifted his hand up to stop me. He nodded to one of his men, and he wheeled Gavin over and placed him beside me, while Xagu sat across from us.

"You must tell me, Aria, how it is that you found us. I am most intrigued by your attempt to save your brother in my camp." Xagu began to eat and didn't seem bothered at all by my attempted rescue of my brother.

"I'd do anything for my family." I kept my head toward my plate, uncomfortable with his question. I dreaded where this conversation could lead as I eyed the ropes that were just on my wrists.

Gavin took my lead and kept his head down as he shoveled food in his mouth.

"Do you understand the agreement that we have?" Xagu replied in a calm, creepy voice. His eyes were on me as I ate.

"You want me to get to Beru." I used his name to shock Xagu. I wanted him to think that Beru had told me more than he did.

"You've spoken to him since we last met. He's told you his name," Xagu said as he sat back and placed his utensils on the table.

"Briefly." I continued eating the meat that was on my plate.

"I have to say, Aria, I am surprised at this and very happy with how far you have come as a dreamwalker so quick." Xagu raised his glass in my direction and then drank.

I dug my fork into my potatoes and shoved them in my mouth, enabling me to not respond.

"We have followed many dreamwalkers. You showed the most potential."

"What are your intentions with holding Gavin?" I asked as soon as my mouth was empty. If he wanted answers, so did I.

"I give you my word that he will be taken care of, and I will see to it personally that it is done right." Xagu waved his hand toward the door. His human walked over to fill his cup. She was aware of his every need.

"She will be your primary caretaker from now on, Gavin. I hope you can forgive your treatment thus far?" Xagu held up his drink in Gavin's direction.

Gavin nodded, then Xagu drank from his glass.

"Will you tell me how Beru is doing?" Xagu changed the subject.

"He's been attacked in some kind of prison." I hoped by answering his questions, Gavin and I would make it out of this tent alive.

"Yes. You are unaware of the circumstances?"

"Yes. As I mentioned, we didn't have much time together. But he is weak." I drank from my cup.

"I expected they wouldn't be treated as just," Xagu said somewhat under his breath.

"I want you to let my brother go now. I'll still help you." I asked the unreasonable as I was the only connection between him and Beru.

"We both know that I am unable to do that. Getting to Beru is something bigger than either of us. This camp and its people exist because of Beru." Xagu settled back into his meal.

"What do I need to do now that I have made contact with Beru?" My face flushed with redness, something I couldn't control.

"You must free Beru, and in return, I will free Gavin." Xagu nodded his head toward me.

"How can I free him, I don't even know how to get to him without dreaming." My voice raised at the impossible task he asked of me.

"I will help you." Xagu took another drink and emptied his glass. He placed it on the edge of the table, and his human practically tripped over herself to refill it.

"You need another dreamwalker. I barely know anything about it," I said, frustrated at him for not letting us go.

"Beru has chosen you," Xagu said calmly.

"He didn't even know who I was."

"Trust the process. How can I help?" Xagu sat back and placed his napkin on the table. Two ur'gel came out of nowhere and cleared his plates.

"I don't know how to dreamwalk. It just happens." I looked around to see who was listening in on our conversations. Dreamwalking felt personal to me, and I wasn't comfortable talking about it with people or ur'gel.

"I have faith that you can harness it. You have proven to be very efficient." Xagu leaned in to listen to me.

"I am seeking out another dreamwalker. In Western March. I was headed there when we came upon your camp."

"Please let me send some of my men with you. It's D'ahvol territory, as you well know. You shouldn't be alone in your travels." Xagu waved his arm again, not waiting on my reply.

"No." I leaned forward, putting my hand out for the ur'gel not to approach our table.

"He will ensure your safety." Xagu acted confused at my reluctance.

"I have someone traveling with me," I replied.

"And they let you get captured by my people?" Xagu raised his eyebrows and sat back in his chair.

"Well, she left me. But only because she said I'm stupid to try to rescue Gavin here." I regretted my words as soon as I saw Xagu in a full belly laugh.

"You would do well to listen to your friend. She is a wise woman."

"Yes, she is." I smiled at his comment.

"I will leave you for a few moments with your brother. I'll gather more provisions for you. My men searched your bags, and I think we can do better." Xagu got up from the table.

I stood and shook his large hand and remembered how I once thought it would take my life. How things can change. Xagu left the tent, and all his people followed him.

"You can't trust him Aria," Gavin said as soon as they left the room. "And what is all this talk about dreamwalking?"

"I just learned I could dreamwalk. Apparently other people knew what I was, Mother Ofburg had intentions of teaching me but...." My voice drifted off at the thought of my last conversation with her. Thoughts of Noble followed until Gavin snapped his fingers.

"Are you doing it now?" Gavin asked, wide-eyed.

"No, stupid." I half laughed at him. "I can't control when it happens. It just happens."

"What is this Beru guy like?"

"He's okay for being beaten and barely eating for two hundred plus years." I thought about our last encounter. The closeness of our bodies. One thing Xagu would not know.

"What will happen when Beru is free?" Gavin wheeled his chair to face me.

"I don't know. I get you back." I pinched his arm.

"Is that worth what could happen?" Gavin's eyebrows lowered, and his eyes hid partially under their lids.

"Of course it is. You will go home, Gavin, and live." I placed my hands on the arms of his chair. I needed him to want to live for himself, not for me.

"Don't do this for me." Gavin grabbed my arms and pulled them toward him. "Your life is more important."

"Don't say that." I tried to hide the tears that wanted to form. His words shocked me.

"I'm in a wheelchair. I'm limited. That's all that I mean. I've heard the tales of what can happen to dreamwalkers." Gavin released my arms.

We both took a moment and finished our meal in silence. Neither of us attempted conversation.

Xagu entered the tent, and two of his men followed and placed bags in the middle of the floor.

"Please, take what you wish." Xagu pointed toward the items.

I nodded, and Gavin remained at the table, not paying us any attention.

"Did I interrupt anything?" Xagu caught on to our disagreement.

"No. We're just saying our goodbyes." I smiled, not wanting Xagu to worry about a sibling feud. I needed him to think I was at his beck and call so

Gavin would be treated well for as long as his stay would be.

I got down on my knees as I looked at the items Xagu had provided. Much better than I had packed, maybe even better than Sade's kit.

"Are you sure I can't send one of my men with you?" Xagu asked again, concern in his voice.

"No, but thank you for the offer and for these items. They will be very useful." I used an empty pack Xagu had provided and loaded it as full as I could get.

"I will need to know when you speak with Beru again." Xagu put his arm around my shoulder so that no one heard our conversation.

"I'll send word when I can." I nodded, unsure if I would follow through.

"I also need you to tell Beru we are going to free him and that you are part of this plan. I need him to trust you."

"That will take a few visits."

"You must manage him. That will be no easy task. I'm sure you are more familiar with what his life is like these days than I, but he wasn't always like that. Please keep that in mind and have patience with him."

This mission was important to him, even though I didn't have the full picture. I got that from his tone.

"I'll try my best." I searched his face for answers, but I didn't even have the questions.

"Tell no one of your mission. There are creatures out there that will stop you if you do."

"Why would they stop me?" Who would want to stop me from talking to someone in a dream?

"I promise, I will tell you more when you need to know more." Xagu nodded to his human. She brought us over two glasses of wine.

"May I toast to your trip?" Xagu held up his glass.

I nodded my head and clinked my glass on his, and we both downed our drinks, as I didn't want to insult his hospitality.

"I should be on my way now." I turned to Gavin, who twisted away. He sat in his chair with a wicked look on his face, angry I was going along with this plan.

"I love you." I walked toward him and kissed him on the forehead.

Gavin turned his head, and I stepped back and gave him one last look over.

"I'll see you soon." As I turned, his hand reached out for me. I leaned back in, and we hugged each other for a few moments.

"Do this for Denny too." Gavin wiped his runny nose with his sleeve.

"We'll avenge him. One plan at a time." I nodded and wiped my own tears away.

I walked toward the door, making sure not to look back.

"What will happen to Gavin if I don't make it?" I asked Xagu as we exited the tent.

"I will make sure he gets home. And I will look after your family."

I believed him in that moment. I had to. He knew what I was giving up by taking on this task for him.

"Thank you."

Xagu walked me to the edge of the woods, where not that long ago I thought Gavin and I would be free and I wouldn't have to free Beru.

"Take care of yourself." Xagu stopped at the edge.

"I will. I hope Beru will believe me. This is a bit far-fetched," I said.

"You will earn his trust. I have no fear of this. I hope this dreamwalker you seek will be able to help you on this journey." Xagu fidgeted with his hands. "You're our only connection to Beru in over two hundred years, Aria."

I nodded in acknowledgment. Xagu gave me one sharp nod, then turned his back and retreated to his tent. I gave the camp one more look then headed off by myself to find the dreamwalker.

Blue light shone from above as I shifted my path to follow Gleet, the moon closest to Lynia and thought of as male. Gleet dominated the sky compared to the white moon Aupra, which we referred to as female. As Gleet was in the southern horizon, I would use him as a guide to navigate my way to the Western March.

My feet ached as they trudged through brush, streams, and forest. Not long into my walk it was clear I had gotten lost. Not one thing was familiar. The brush was untouched by human or creature with no paths to be seen.

Darkness surrounded me. Every crack and chirp made me jump from my heightened fear of being alone. I dug deeper to remember everything I had learned about surviving in the wilderness. It wasn't long before it rushed back to me. A lot of people depended on me, and I had no intention of letting them down.

Rocks skidded below me as my feet stumbled along. My eyes roamed for any indication of anything living. Signs were rare in the forest, but some locals did use them. The warmth of the sun hit my face and took away the chillness the darkness had induced.

I kept a steady pace as I once again prayed to whichever Gods would be listening that my navigation wasn't completely off. I found what appeared to be a path and made my way toward it. I wanted to do a dance when I found the path, but I was still uncertain where it led. It provided relief, but only briefly as someone whistled in the distance. Excitement grew at the idea of having company once again, however, that disappeared as the dangers I had been warned against came to mind. Ducking behind a large tree, I waited for who or what was headed my way.

A young man, I couldn't tell if he was part creature or not from the distance that I was from him, whistled as he walked or rather danced down the path. He didn't look dangerous. I giggled at his silliness. The boy stopped, startled, and shook his head back and forth looking around. He'd heard me.

"Is anybody there?" He tiptoed further on the path searching for someone.

I stepped out from behind the tree slowly as not to alarm him.

"Hello?" I called to him but kept my distance. He stood still, glancing me up and down to determine my fretfulness.

"Hello. Why do you look lost? It's not a safe place in the forest." He walked closer to me at a slower pace.

"I'm trying to find my way to Western March, but I'm afraid I've gotten myself lost." I hoped he would confirm the correct direction.

"Why, you're not lost at all. I'm going that way right now." His body loosened up as he approached me.

"Would you mind a tagalong?" I asked coyly.

He stood there for a moment and shrugged his shoulders. "Sure, why not. Astor Dell at your service." He bowed to me like a character in a play.

I couldn't help but giggle again. He wasn't much taller than I and had longer brown, wavy hair that just reached his nose. He was rather thin and wore a green velvet coat that appealed to his vanity. He was unlike anyone I had ever met. I guessed we would get along fine.

"Aria Trevil." I offered my hand.

He skipped over to shake it.

"Apprentice wizard at your service, madam." He winked at me, and I got the feeling he was quite the little flirt.

"May I ask why you are going to Western March?" I asked as we walked down the path together.

"I'm going to meet my master there. Well, I hope so, anyway." Astor skipped along, and I quickened my pace to keep up with his stride.

"Do you mean he may not be there?" I was curious about his story.

"Oh no, he's there. It's more a matter of if he will see me," Astor said with a sheepish grin that immediately made me want to know more.

"I think there is a story here." I laughed, and Astor laughed with me.

"I'm afraid I may have gone overboard just one too many times. But isn't that the job of an apprentice? I'm sure he won't be mad long. He never is." Astor stopped in front of me. "Now your story?"

"I'm a Healer. I'm going to Western March to speak to someone to help me with the situation I'm in." I walked past him. While I was at ease with Astor, I wasn't sure how much of a secret keeper he would be.

"Sounds like a good story to me." Astor skirted past and jumped in front of me to stop. "Scorned lover?" He asked dramatically.

His silliness again made me smile. I had known many people who possessed the ability to perform magic, and it was easy to see how Astor could get himself in trouble with his personality.

"Certainly not." I gave him a side-eye as I passed him again. "Are we going on this journey together?" I joked as he stood there and watched me walk further up the path.

"A passionate crush that you would give your life up for?" He caught up with me and dramatically flung his arms about.

"None of the above. It's rather boring. You have a much better story than I." I knew instantly this would not be a silent walk. Astor loved the limelight and any attention he received. And I needed a good laugh.

Astor fidgeted in his pocket and pulled out a small carving of a dragon. He held it up for me to see. "Is this lovely lady going to meet her destiny in Western March?"

"What are you doing?" My eyebrows squinted with curiosity.

“Ever since I was a wee one, I've always wanted a dragon to be bonded with, but that’s not meant to be. So I improvised.” Astor bowed again and lifted his hand with the small dragon. He gestured for me to take it.

I picked it up, not wanting to be rude and also because I was curious. The small dragon was meticulously carved out of stone. There were several spots that were worn down, and I could tell he had carried this dragon with him for a very long time.

“It's very beautiful.” I handed it back to him. As our hands touched, I was able to see another side of him, his loneliness. The reason for him being so outgoing and foolish.

“Thank you. He accompanies me everywhere.” Astor smiled at me and placed his dragon safely back in his pocket. “Do you have any treasures you carry with you?”

“A rock. My brother gave it to me. It's supposed to castaway fools.” I smiled at my brother's superstitions.

“Well, you can tell him it didn't work.” Astor smiled mischievously at me.

“I see they didn’t kill you,” a voice called from behind us.

We both turned toward the voice.

Astor fumbled with his coat tails as he tried to retrieve something from his pocket.

After a few cracks from the woods, Sade stepped out onto the trail.

“It's okay. She’s my guide.” I looked toward Astor, who was holding up a brittle stick for protection.

“A guide who left you for dead?” Astor was confused as he glanced between Sade and me.

“I left her because she’s stupid.” Sade joined us. “So, what happened? I don't see Gavin.”

“Gavin is safe for now. They gave me their word. This is Astor Dell, a wizard. Astor, this is Sade Lemm, a great warrior wolf,” I introduced them.

The two new friends shook hands with uneasiness. We were an unlikely clan, but our chances of making it to Western March together were now greater.

“Will you join us?” I hoped indeed she would.

Sade shrugged her shoulders. “I guess.” Then walked between us up the path. “As long as you don't slow me down.”

Astor shook his head, still confused. “You two are friends? On purpose?”

“I wouldn't go quite that far.” I linked arms with him, and we caught up with Sade, who walked much faster.

“Going to get dark soon. We need to pick up the pace.” Sade glanced back, smiling. I wasn't sure what she thought of Astor.

We walked for several minutes in silence as Astor seemed uncomfortable in Sade’s presence. I’d have to break the ice between them, but Astor beat me to it.

“So part wolf, you said. That’s an interesting combination. White wolf, I would presume.”

“How did you know that?” I hadn't picked up on that.

“My studies. It was her hair that gave it away. I'm not just a pretty face,” Astor said with a jester’s smile.

I laughed at his antics, but I was anxious for him and Sade to bond.

“You say you’re a wizard?” Sade stopped and turned abruptly back to us and looked him over with an odd expression on her face. Sometimes it was difficult to know what she was thinking.

“Why, yes, a deeply talented wizard, I may add,” Astor replied as he stood at attention.

Sade rolled her eyes. “What are you doing in the middle of the woods?” Sade directed her question to Astor.

“I just so happen to be on the hunt to find my master.” I sensed a tinge of anger in his response.

“You don't have a master, do you?” Sade folded her arms.

“That's just a technicality.” Astor hung his head low to his right side.

“I like you,” Sade said matter-of-factly, then turned on her heels and continued to walk.

Astor shook his head with confusion and then began to follow her. This little clan would be all right.

“And why are you going to Western March, Ms. Sade?” Astor jumped to her side.

“You could say I have some unfinished business.” Sade walked past him and didn’t bother to turn to talk to us.

“Sounds ominous. I'd like to get in on that.” Astor ran to catch up to her.

I smiled to myself about having both of them on this journey. Sade, the protector, and Astor, the jester.

“I'm betting you would.” Sade smirked at him.

"I'm always up for an adventure. Would anyone have any food they could spare?" Astor's head bobbed between Sade and me.

"Let's find a spot to make camp. It's about that time." Sade veered off into the woods.

Astor and I followed as she found the perfect campsite.

We all settled in and did our part to set up the camp. We'd only be here for a quick bite to eat and rest our feet. We still had a few days' worth of travel and might need to stop frequently if we ran into more ur'gel.

As we sat around the camp, Astor dug into his food as soon as it was plated.

Sade and I watched in amusement and partly disgust as he used his fingers to shovel the food into his mouth as quickly as possible.

Sade's lips pressed together as her eyes narrowed.

"What do you think of him?" I leaned in toward her with no worries Astor would hear us over his loud eating.

"He's easy to get rid of if we need to."

My eyes narrowed as I thought about what she meant by "get rid of."

“I’m joking.” Sade laughed.

“On another note, I wanted to ask you if you could give me some tips on fighting. I'd like to learn from you on this journey.” I focused on Sade and hoped with Astor sitting next to us maybe she would give in and help me.

“Well, I’m not much of a fighter. More of a lover if you need help in that category,” Astor joked and winked my way.

“Oh, she sucks in that category too,” Sade shot back with a giggle.

“I do not,” I tried to defend myself, but she was right. I had never even been kissed.

“You’re good at almost dying.” Sade turned to Astor and nodded.

“Now that's a story I want to hear.” Astor moved between Sade and me and waited for one of us to continue.

“I’m never going to hear the end of this.” I shook my head.

“Nope.” Sade dug into her rice. “That’s a nice kit that the ur’gel packed for you.”

“Ur’gel?” Astor practically dropped his plate.

“They have her brother,” Sade said without any emotion. It was easy for her to give away my secrets.

“That’s not up for discussion.” I felt betrayed. It wasn’t up to her to tell that story, just like it wasn’t up to me to tell hers.

“You've touched a sore spot.” Astor dug back into his food. “You ladies are feisty. You know how to push each other's buttons.”

Sade and I peered at each other. I had certainly said things I regretted to her.

“I'm sorry,” Sade muttered from under her breath, averting any eye contact with me. I figured she never apologized, so I recognized the rare moment.

“Thank you.” I didn’t want to make her apology a big thing. We were both on the same page, and no words were needed.

“Well then, that’s easy.” Astor grinned to himself.

We sat around the camp a bit longer than we should have, but we all needed a good laugh and Astor provided that. He goofed around and made fun of himself with little hesitation. Sade even contributed with her quick, smart wit.

This journey just got a little bit brighter.

Exhaustion seeped through me as we walked for several days. We were wet and worn out. Sade had wanted to push forward, but Astor and I convinced her to stop after a deer passed us in the woods. We were in desperate need of protein to get us through the last leg of this trip.

Astor and I stayed back to set up camp as Sade took to the woods in search of the deer.

"She's a wonder." Astor dropped a bunch of branches by the fire.

"She's a hard shell to crack, but when you do, it's worth it." I sat back on the ground and rubbed two dry sticks together. Once I had a spark, I leaned over and blew on the flame. It caught quickly as I added dry kindling. Sade had shown me a couple of different ways to create fire, and I had taken a liking to this manner.

"You know, I could do that with magic." Astor sat down across from me.

"I know." I added more wood to my masterpiece. "But I won`t always have the Great Astor with me."

"You're getting quicker. Sade wouldn't tell you that, though, even if she thinks it." Astor lay back on the grass and looked up to the sky.

I smiled to myself. It didn't take him long to figure out the real Sade. I had enjoyed myself with Astor along for the trip. Sade let loose more and wasn't as cynical.

"I'm not supposed to say anything, but we heard you last night." Astor rolled over on his side and played with some strands of grass, avoiding eye contact with me.

The skin on my face started to burn. The heat rose from my neck to my cheeks. I'd seen Beru every few nights. I'd chosen for most visits not to let him see me so I could study him. I had no control over when I dreamwalked.

"It sounded heated." He plucked some grass and threw it in my direction.

"It wasn't," I lied. There was something between us. His mind attracted me. He was assertive and knew what he wanted. I admired him. I looked forward to each dream and wished for him each night.

"Do you know about his family?" Astor sat up and looked around us.

"No." I had wondered about his life before prison, but it wasn't my focus.

"So, I may have been holding out on you a little bit." Astor rocked on his side. I just knew he was itching to tell me something.

"Go on." I remained in my position and lifted my eyes to him. I tamed my eagerness from showing.

"I've heard of Beru from my master." Astor flinched, putting his hand over his face.

I didn't move. I was scared to show any excitement from learning more about him. I had wanted this for a while, yet now I didn't seem ready.

"Okay," was all I could muster. I focused on breaking the little branches of the larger limbs Astor brought over and placed them in the fire. "I'm ready."

"It's more on the personal side. About his life at home." Astor watched my expression.

"Spill it." I wanted to know everything, and I needed to know before Sade returned.

"He was married." Astor made a long, dramatic pause.

"Yes," I replied and tried not to show that it bothered me. It had always been a possibility, but it stung. Not that Beru and I had something going on. Just a few close encounters.

"His wife and child were murdered the night before he was captured," Astor said, again very dramatically.

"Did he know about the murder?" I shook my head in embarrassment. How would Astor have known? No one had seen Beru since he'd been captured.

"One can only guess." Astor settled back into his regular tone of voice.

"How did your master know?" I kept feeding the fire to ensure it was hot enough for cooking when Sade returned. Also to hide my interest in Astor's story.

"There's more talk of the war in Western March. It lives on." Astor's face was grim.

"Not like Low Forest?" No one spoke about the war there. My father's stories were how I knew the little bit that I did, and they were altered to tell a child. As we got older, my father spoke less about it.

"No, Low Forest wants to forget what happened. If you grew up in Western March, the stories are passed down from generation to generation." Astor sat up and helped me break more branches for the fire.

"Do you know any more about Beru?" I tried to act like I didn't care. Astor was the first person that knew anything about him that would speak. I learned more from him than I had learned with all my time with Beru.

"No. That's all I got."

A noise in the woods caught our attention. We both stood and surveyed the edge, waiting for whatever it was to come out.

Dizziness took over as the thought of having to protect Astor and myself without Sade seemed like a long shot. Especially on such little sleep. My head shot toward where Astor was focused, and relief filled me when I saw Sade standing with a deer hoisted on her shoulders.

"Anyone hungry?" Sade dumped his body on the ground.

Astor and I grinned ear to ear. The last time I had a full meal had been in Xagu's tent.

Astor helped Sade clean the body as I heated the pans so they would be ready cook.

We scarfed down our meal and opened a bottle of wine Xagu had given me for the trip.

"Okay, so you're not so bad now with tracking." Sade recounted to Astor how I had gotten us lost in Low Forest.

"I managed just fine," I replied with a mouth full of food.

"You're okay." Sade filled her plate with more meat.

"Even I learned a few techniques for fighting in your lesson to Aria," Astor revealed, falling off his log, pretending to be dead.

"If all else fails."

"Play dead," I added.

We were overtired and needed this break.

Astor stood and walked toward the woods and relieved himself.

"We don't need to see that," I called after him.

"I can't see anything." Sade smiled at me and we broke out into giggles.

"I think he's off to bed." I turned as he collapsed into our makeshift cabin.

"I'd say we will hear the snoring shortly."

I returned to my plate, eager to finish up and rest as well.

"I'm glad we're alone." Sade's tone implied we'd be having a serious conversation.

"Is there something you want to talk about?"

"You mentioned seeing Beru a few more times. Just interested in what you found out." Sade seemed genuinely interested. These past few days together had brought a different understanding between us.

"It's different each time." I stared at my plate. My time with Beru seemed private, between him and I, but I owed Sade some explanations for being my guide.

"How so?" Sade put her empty plate down, got comfortable in her spot, and gave me her full attention.

"I don't always show myself to him, not that I can't. I sometimes don't feel like I should." It was hard to explain why that made sense to me.

"So, you watch him?" Sade tilted her head to the left.

"I guess I like him better when he can't see me. He's more himself." I tried to explain it the best way that I could.

"What is he like when you show yourself?"

"It's almost as if he has something to prove. Although I'm certain sometimes when I don't show myself, he knows that I'm there." I wrapped my blanket around my shoulders. I hadn't the courage to ask him why he did that.

"Maybe he doesn't want a reminder of the living," Sade guessed.

"It's like I can't turn him off sometimes. I just want to sleep, but I can't stay away either." I let my guard down. It was good to be able to talk to someone about this.

"Is that a dreamwalking thing? Getting attached to someone?" Sade threw another log on the fire.

"Could be." I hoped that wasn't the case. I wondered if he thought about me as much as I did him. Or was he thinking of his wife?

"You look sad when you talk about him," Sade commented.

"I just question my part in this. It's exhausting." Tears wanted to form, but I thought of Gavin being home with my parents and happy moments.

I ran my hand through my thick, dirty hair, how I wanted to bathe in a tub so desperately. The thought of bathing reminded me of a dreamwalk where Beru had been soaking in a tub. I hadn't made myself known, but his body stiffened as I walked closer to him. I stopped, embarrassed he had seen me watching him, but then he dunked his whole body under the water and carried on as if I wasn't there. My cheeks flushed as I closed my eyes to bring me back to that moment.

"I'm going to bed." Sade got up. "It looks like you won't be far behind."

"I'll just be a few minutes," I watched her walk back to where Astor was already sleeping.

It had been a while since I'd been alone. As I sat in front of the warm fire, my thoughts turned to Beru again. I couldn't get him out of my mind and almost wanted to sleep more on the chance of seeing him again.

I placed another log on the fire and went to join Astor and Sade to get some sleep.

The next morning, Sade let Astor and I sleep in a little bit. She went off into the woods to scout out our next route. She also needed time to herself. She was used to working alone.

We got ourselves up and ate breakfast. I had thought Sade would be back before we'd be done. However, she had not returned, so we focused on breaking down camp. We packed our bags and tore down our shelter. We made it so no one would ever know we had camped there.

"I'm getting worried." Astor shoved the last of our things in a pack.

We hadn't seen her leave in the early morning, so we didn't know which way she had gone.

"Me too. She should have been back by now." I searched the ground to see if I could find any of her footprints, but we had been working on the camp all morning, and we had destroyed any chance we'd had to track her.

"Do you think she would leave us?" Astor reached my side and stared off into the woods where I had been looking.

"Sade wouldn't do that," I said, not so sure of my answer. I didn't want Astor to worry.

"Yeah, she wouldn't." Astor rubbed his hand up and down my arm, then went back to our packs and sat down.

Astor and I stayed in camp and waited for Sade to return. The worst thoughts ran through our minds that Sade either had left us or something bad had happened to her. My hands were numb as I rubbed the handle of my bag, waiting for her to come out of the woods and yell at us for losing more daylight.

"She's not coming back." Astor lay back and placed his hat over his face to keep the sun from burning his rather pale skin.

"She'll be back," I replied through gritted teeth. I hated he might be right. No sooner than I had that thought, we could hear someone walking toward us in the woods. Astor shot up from his position and grabbed me by the arm as he tried to pull me back.

"You look like you saw a ghost." Sade trampled right past us to pick up her pack.

"Where did you go?"

"Western March. It's just through those trees."

"Why didn't you wake us?" I questioned her, confused at why she never told us we were this close.

"You needed the rest." Sade shifted her shoulders to get her pack just right before we left camp.

We gathered our belongings and followed Sade though the woods. I didn't bother to hide my excitement to see this land I had heard of from a young age.

We began our last leg, and soon we faced the base of the mountains. We traveled along the edge of the Oubliee Desert. The heat scorched my skin as did the sand that was being whipped around in the wind. We had little coverage.

All three of us had to be on alert for any Oubliee. They were human nomads who ruled the desert of the Northwestern Territory. We were guarded, as the thought of fighting them or any creature at this point, would quickly end us.

Time passed slowly in the desert. Our feet sank deep into the hot sand. We walked for most of the day and welcomed the sun going down. Just as I was almost unable to go any further, the lights of Western March appeared.

It was the most beautiful sight I had ever seen. The mountain hung at a slant, and a small piece of rock magically kept it upright. The temperature dropped, and large pieces of ice hung off the slanted sides of the mountain. The higher up the mountain, the more lights you could see. I closed my eyes to rest them and was daunted at the thought we had to climb it.

“There it is.” Sade walked past me, then stopped to take in the beauty.

“Home,” Astor said from behind me.

“Let’s take a break while it’s dark and head up first thing.” Sade pulled off to the side where the rocky part of the mountain would provide us with some shelter from the blowing sand.

Astor followed her and took off his boots as we reached the cave and turned them upside down to empty the sand.

I stood there a few more moments and stared at the mountain. I hadn't thought of this moment. There had been too many possibilities that we wouldn't make it. Tomorrow morning, I would meet the dreamwalker and learn how I could free Beru.

At daybreak, we ate and started to break camp to head up the mountain. Astor was eager to find his master, and today I would meet the dreamwalker. My hands shook as I packed my bag. So much depended on this meet, and it needed to go according to plan.

"This is the day you have been waiting for," Astor stated as we set out.

"I hope I'm prepared for it," I uttered as I tried to keep stride with him and Sade.

It wasn't long before we could see the city's edge. As we entered, it didn't look like I had expected. There was a vast array of people everywhere. As we walked past the merchants, the offerings were plenty, and many of the items I had never seen before. The merchants shouted out to you with their wares as you passed by their booths.

Sade stopped to purchase some fresh fruit. Her lump of silver delivered more food than if she had paid the same in Low Forest.

"Pick your jaw up." Sade elbowed me and threw an apple toward me, then at Astor. I brought it to my nose to smell. It was sweeter. I ate it rather quickly, thankful for something other than rice.

"We aren't far from where my master is. It's just up this way." Astor pushed past us to lead.

The buildings were partially made from sand and mud. The windows were simple holes, and the winds blew through to keep the building cool. The buildings were very old and had stood longer than our village in Low Forest. They were stacked side by side, each house sharing a wall with the next. Most of the homes had a vending station outside their front door. It seemed common to even see children at the helm, calling out to peasants as they walked by.

Astor walked faster than he had the whole journey and didn't partake in any talk. His lips moved as he mumbled under his breath.

"I could have sworn it's around here." Astor stopped and spun around, looking from building to building. He began to breathe faster, and if I hadn't known him, I would have thought he was in the midst of a panic attack.

"There." Sade pointed toward a building.

Astor turned and nodded his head, but he didn't move toward it.

Sade must have been right in choosing the building.

"That's it." Astor nodded his head but didn't move.

"Let's go." Sade pushed Astor forward with the palm of her hand to his back.

He stumbled forward in slow motion.

Sade pounded on the door.

Astor reached his hand out for her arm to pull her away, but he wasn't quick enough.

A little slot on the door opened, and a pair of eyes appeared. The slot closed again. Silence.

"Idok, please. I have come to be of service. I promise no more antics." Astor leaned against the door and raised his voice.

I moved my hand to my mouth to hide my giggles as poor Astor tried his best to get his master to open the door.

"And I'm sorry about your hair. I'm certain it will grow back," Astor alleged. He turned his head back to Sade as if he had hoped we hadn't heard him.

"Go away." Idok's fist pounded on the inside of the door.

"I will not," Astor insisted. "You were assigned as my mentor, and I will follow you wherever you go."

Astor, Sade, and I stared at the door as we waited for Idok's response. Poor Astor, he hadn't much of a choice if his master decided to abandon him. He would be shunned and forced to learn and practice on his own. Astor may be a bit dopey, but he could be reined in.

The door opened, and an older man appeared. He wore a long red cotton robe that hid his pudgy figure the best it could. Most noticeable was his bald head. I gasped toward Astor, who appeared just as shocked as I was.

"It will not grow back," Idok remarked through gritted teeth.

"Not even with your magic?" Astor cowered.

"You're an idiot, Astor," Idok specified as he stood back and gestured for us all to enter the building.

Sade and I followed Astor's lead as he nodded and walked inside.

The house was well decorated, likely by a female. The colors were muted, and most of his belongings matched the same color scheme.

"May I offer you beverages?" Idok held his hands together and kept an eye on Astor.

"Yes, please."

Sade nodded, and just as Astor opened his mouth to reply, Idok left to get our drinks.

"His hair?" Sade smirked.

"I'm sure something can be done about it." Astor rubbed the front of his jacket.

It was odd seeing him like this, a ball of nerves as he waited on what his master would say to him.

"Here you are." Idok entered the room with a tray and two drinks. "Please, have a seat."

Idok smiled at Sade and me as we took our drinks from his tray.

We sat on the luxurious couch next to its matching chairs. I'd never been in a place so fancy before. We sat in silence for a few moments. I gathered that Idok hadn't had many visitors based on how uncomfortable he sat.

"That's a beautiful lampshade," I pointed out as I tried to ease the tension

Out of the corner of my eye, I could see Astor as he shook his head no at me.

“My dear Beulif made it,” Idok sobbed as he pulled a cloth from his pocket and wiped his eyes, then blew his nose. “She’s passed on now.”

“I’m so sorry.” As I reached for him, Sade placed her hand on my leg. I leaned back in my chair.

“Maybe we should go and leave you two to chat.” Sade stood, and I followed her.

“Yes, we can catch up later.” Astor stood and placed his hand on Idok’s back to comfort him.

Sade left the room and headed for the front door.

“I’ll see you later,” I whispered to Astor, and he nodded.

“You can’t show sympathy,” Sade said as soon as we were outside.

“I’m sorry. I didn’t know feeling sorry for someone was bad.”

“It’s a sign of weakness for him to cry in public. It could be costly for him as a magician.”

“Noted.” That didn’t take away any sadness I had for Idok. He missed his wife and wasn’t allowed to mourn her. The first thing I didn’t like about Western March. I speculated what else I would do wrong here.

"We are about an hour's walk from the dreamwalker." Sade entered an alley of markets. It was different than the ones we had just seen. Businesses owned them rather than families. The goods were more expensive, and they had more variety. I bet Idok and Beulif purchased most of the items for their house from here.

I made notes of items I would purchase and bring home to Mother. She deserved the best. Father may not have been able to give it to her, but I would sure try.

As we made our way to the end of the alley, people shouted ahead of us. Sade's arm shot out in front of me.

"What is it?" I couldn't tell which direction the noise had come from.

"Just up ahead. D'ahvol perhaps. They aren't the friendliest," Sade whispered.

We walked toward the noise, eyes following us as we passed each booth. Most in the city would know we were here by now.

As we exited the alley, it was clear where the noises had originated from. We had almost stepped into the middle of a confrontation going on between a few creatures. One caught my eye as he stood seven feet tall and carried an ax and sword on his back. His eyes drifted toward us, and he stood stiff-backed.

"Umm, Sade," I practically used her as a shield. She tried her best to shake me off as the large man made his way toward us.

"Let me talk," Sade cautioned.

"Well, what do we have here?" the thing beckoned as his heavy feet stomped the ground.

"Just passing through." Sade met him eye to eye, not a quiver in her body.

"A wolf and a—" His eyes floated to me as they squinted, trying to decipher my magic talent.

"Healer," Sade offered, as I nodded and tried to look the part.

"A wolf and a healer in Western March." The thing laughed as he glanced back at the creature he had just verbally attacked.

I could feel myself getting light-headed. We were outnumbered, and I was no match for any of these creatures. I glanced at Sade, but her cool gaze was trained on him.

"A warrior picking on innocents," Sade quipped back at him.

"You know a thing or two about me white wolf?" He shoved his hands under his belt, amused.

"I know who you are, just as you know who I am." Sade grinned, daring him.

What was she doing? Making this large thing mad?

"And what do you know of me?" he grumbled as he placed his hand on the handle of his sword.

"You're Iri Gueust, Warrior for Hire," Sade expressed her disdain in his line of work.

"You mean merchant guard. To protect the lands from people like you." Iri spat on the ground, inches from Sade's foot.

While Sade was well versed in fighting, I was not sure her tactics of egging Iri on were in our best interest. They stood face to face, minus the height, ready to spar at a moment's notice. The more they bantered, the less the chance of being able to walk past these brutes.

"We are just passing through." I shuddered as I tried to walk past him, but that just refocused his attention on me.

"A healer, you say." His voice expressed distrust at our story. "I have someone in need of healing."

I turned toward Sade, but it was no use. She was ready to fight if need be. I needed to charm our way out of here alone.

"I could take a look at them once we are done." I adjusted my back and stood tall. I remembered Sade told me part of fighting is psychological. If you could make yourself seem like a threat, do so to prevent a battle. Adrenaline pumped through my veins as Iri stared me down.

"Now," he warned, spit flying from the sides of his mouth.

I nodded as I hoped Sade would chime in. However, she remained quiet with her eyes on Iri's weapons.

"I have an emergency, and we must go as quickly as possible." I tried to walk past him again, but he stepped back in my direction, stopping me again.

"Where is the emergency?" Iri held out his hand for me to stop moving.

"It's none of your business," Sade retorted from behind him.

Iri lifted his sword above his head, and Sade grabbed her sword from her side to fight.

"A dreamwalker," I yelled as I stepped in between them with one hand in each of their directions, hoping to stop the insanity of this fight. "I need to see a dreamwalker."

"Dreamwalker, you say?" Iri's forehead shrunk as he stepped closer to me.

I froze and regretted what I had just revealed. I should have left the talking to Sade. I backed up but tried not to let fear show on my face.

Iri matched my steps and grabbed me by the arm as he pulled me away from Sade's protection.

"What dreamwalker?"

Iri's voice rumbled in my ears as I cowered and waited for Sade to intervene.

"I... I..." I stuttered, unable to speak.

"Aria," Sade called from behind me.

Iri's head swung back toward Sade then to me again. "You're Aria?" he asked.

"Yes," I declared, still cowering.

He let go of my arm and stood back at attention like he was my warrior now.

"I'll take you to him." Iri held his arm out for me.

I turned to Sade, who appeared just as confused as I was. I nodded as I took his arm. I prayed he was on our side as I blindly followed him.

Iri was a man of his word and took us straight to Svan. We arrived at his home, which was off a lane. We passed by numerous trees, whose branches formed a bridge over the lane. White flowers were in bloom on the branches.

“Will you be okay alone inside?” Sade interrupted my thoughts as we approached the door.

“Yes.” I gestured for her to leave with Iri. I wasn’t afraid to meet him. I lifted my palms up and not one tremble.

I stood back as Iri knocked on the door. He stepped back and took me by the arm as he placed me in front of the door.

An older woman answered the door and Iri nodded at her. She smiled at me and stepped aside so we could go in. We entered an empty large room.

“Wait here.” The older woman walked toward a hallway off the room.

“This place is incredible.” The room’s walls were painted in bright colors and had many carvings. The front of the room hosted a large throne with two smaller chairs off to the side.

"Iri, I trust you to be respectful with Aria's guide," Svan said as he took his seat on the throne.

His voice was deep and soothing. He was a tall man, balding and very thin.

"Of course." Iri bowed and led Sade away toward the door.

"I am very pleased you have come." Svan stood and motioned his hand for me to take my place beside him.

I obliged and settled into the comfortable chair.

As I sat, his servant placed a cup of hot tea next to me.

"Rose tea. To help with the shakes." Svan brought his cup to his lips, then he stopped and shifted toward me. "Do you get the shakes after you dreamwalk?"

"No," I uttered, unsure of the proper manner to address him.

"You must excuse me. I am curious to meet another dreamwalker. As you know, there aren't many of us around." He grinned, and I began to feel at ease.

"I had no idea until recently. About being a dreamwalker," I blurted out as I wanted to tell him everything about my life.

"That's unfortunate." He appeared upset.

"That's why I have come. In hopes that you will teach me to be a good dreamwalker," I said, practically bouncing out of my chair with excitement. However, my mood was not met.

Instead, Svan sat back in his chair and didn't say anything.

"I have been dreaming of you for over a year. Unable to find you." Svan sat still.

I wanted to reply to his comment. However, I sat quietly as he appeared to be deep in thought.

"What did you dream?" I finally asked as I leaned toward him.

"I need to help you on your quest. To do that, I need to know all your knowledge on dreamwalking."

"Not much. I've been doing what I feel is right in the moment," I said, embarrassed.

"Let's start there, shall we?" Svan smiled at me as he gestured to my drink.

I sipped the sweet tea and felt a calming sensation overtake my body. My sore muscles no longer ached, and my skin felt clean and moisturized.

"A little magic always helps." Svan grinned as he set his drink down and nodded for me to finish my drink.

I eagerly obliged.

Svan sat back in his chair, and his hands formed a triangle as he rubbed them back and forth over his mouth.

"Many people are afraid of dreamwalkers," Svan explained, "because of the extraordinary power that comes with it."

I nodded as I listened. I need to remember every bit of advice he offered.

"We are able to enter the world of dreams, in the flesh, as a form of teleportation. I guess that's the easiest way to explain it." He poured more tea into our glasses and dipped a leaf in his glass.

"Thank you," I muttered, not wanting to interrupt, eager for any information he had to offer.

"It makes it easy to spy on people." Svan's voice drifted away, and his eyes glazed over with an old memory. "To make them do what you wish or even kill a person."

Then his eyes turned black. My heart raced as fear bubbled up in my stomach.

"Once you learn to touch, it's hard to turn back."

"Touch?" I asked confused. I had touched many things in my dreams. It was the only way I could get through to Beru.

"Yes, you may or may not be able to touch things in your dream. It's a rarity, but lethal. Only the strongest dreamwalkers are able to. It takes years of training." Svan took another sip from his cup.

"I can touch things," I blurted out, not waiting for him to finish.

Svan took in a deep breath, and his head tilted sideways as he stared at me silently.

Perhaps he didn't believe me.

"So, it is true. I've seen you in my dreams with a man, but his back had always been turned from me." Svan shook his head in disbelief. "Even an old man can be fooled by his dreams."

"It was the only way to communicate with him sometimes."

Svan smiled to himself, and I wondered if he knew the man in my dreams was Beru.

"When I first dreamwalked as a young boy, I often ended up in the buff." He chuckled again to himself. "Those were my learning years. It takes a strong mind to dreamwalk."

"I'm not sure I have that." I grimaced.

"Only time will tell." Svan stood and gestured for me to follow him.

We walked down a hallway. One side of the hall had glass from floor to ceiling. He had many plants and a garden two women were tending to. Once we arrived at the end of the hall, he opened a door and nodded for me to enter.

I walked into the room, which appeared to be his bedroom. I turned back to him as he closed the door.

"This is my studio." Svan walked toward a small table by the bed. He picked up a candle and passed it to me. "For protection. May be superstitious, but I think it helps."

I could smell the lavender in the wax. It reminded me of home.

"Please." Svan motioned for me to lay on the bed.

I walked over with some hesitation, being in a strange man's bedroom, but I still felt comfortable. I climbed up and lay down on my back on the softest bed I had ever used. Svan sat beside me on a chair. He opened a drawer under the side table and took out a sheet of paper and dipped the tip of his feather in some ink.

"There are limitations to dreamwalking." He scribbled on his paper. "We must not affect the real world. If you are injured in a dream, you take that back with you. If you die in a dream, well, you don't come back."

I swallowed hard as I remembered the first time I dreamwalked.

"It is possible to take someone with you on a dreamwalk. It's rarely done and professionally unacceptable, as they are not trained. There have been cases reported of people dying." Svan scribbled on his paper, his eyes trained straight ahead.

What if Svan was dreamwalking right now? He had to be. I was sure if I spoke up, he would not hear me. He was deep in a trance. I peeked over at his page to look at his scribbles. They made no sense. I lay back on the bed and listened while trying to remain calm.

"The hardest lesson is to not stay in the dream too long, for you will stay there forever," Svan's voice changed.

"Svan?" I asked quietly, scared to open my eyes too far.

His head turned to me, and the whites of his eyes reappeared. He didn't look scary anymore.

"Yes."

"Are you ok?" I managed to get the words out of my mouth.

"Yes. But there is one more thing." Svan drew in a long breath. "You can lose your way back to your body."

The thought had never occurred to me. I had always made my way back without trying. My dreams seemed to end, and I had no control over how long I stayed in them.

"If you lose your way, your body is in danger," Svan put his paper back in his drawer with the feather. "I'm too old for this." He smiled as he placed the palm of his hands on the handles of his chair to help lift himself up. He was noticeably weaker.

"Are you ok? Should I call someone?" I sat up to help him stand.

"I am fine, but I will take your arm to go back to the parlor."

I reached over to him and linked our arms together as we walked back to the front room. I helped him sit on his throne.

"Thank you, dear. I don't get around to dreamwalking much. It takes the life out of you." Svan smiled as he joked with me.

I could feel the weakness getting stronger each time I dreamwalked. I wasn't certain as to what caused it and tried my best to ignore it.

"My tea please." Svan pointed to where the kettle was.

I poured him a cup of tea, and he drank it down, so I poured him another until the pot was empty. He regained his strength slowly.

"It was an accident." Svan paused.

I watched as Svan gasped for breaths. His long slender fingers stroked his neck as his chest heaved up and down.

"I stayed too long." Svan smiled with sadness.

The mood in the room changed as I waited until he was well enough to tell his story.

"Susana. She was the same age as my daughter. She stayed too long. Her mother traveled from Bruhier." Svan reached for his cup again and drank it down. He picked up his bell and a woman brought out another kettle full.

I didn't rush him. I waited for him to be ready to speak as all kinds of scenarios ran through my mind.

"I found her, but...." His voice drifted off in thought.

"It's not your fault." I wanted him to be happy again.

"It happened because I let it." He sat up in his seat. "Always take responsibility for your actions."

"I will."

"Don't tell people you can dreamwalk. They'll come for you. Some for help. Others to use you." Svan drank more of his miracle tea, and his breathing was noticeably better.

I nodded in understanding, thinking of Xagu and the mission he sent me on.

"Now, is everything all right? Why have you come here, to see me?" Svan reached over and placed his hand on my arm in a grip.

"For your teaching." My neck grew red from lying to him.

"You have a brother in a chair?" Svan removed his hand from my arm.

"Yes." I trembled, thinking of him being held prisoner by the ur'gel, "How did you know?"

"He was also in my dream. He's somewhere he doesn't want to be." Svan squinted as he rested his back on his throne.

My hands were numb as they fell to my side. I didn't notice my feet rocking back and forth from anxiety.

"The ur'gel have him." I couldn't keep it in anymore. Once I told Svan, he had to help me. We were dreamwalkers.

"Xagu and his men?" Svan asked.

"Yes." I hoped he would know what to do.

"What do they want from you?"

I stood and rung my hands, trying to get the feeling back. I paced back and forth debating with myself on telling Svan everything that had happened.

"Aria." Svan raised and took me by my arm as he brought me back to my seat. "We dreamwalkers must stick together."

"They want me to release someone." I took a large gulp. "From a prison."

Svan's jaw tightened. "Have you done as they wished?"

"No. But I have seen the man. Several times."

"And his name is?" Svan asked.

I wanted to say that I didn't know his name. I wanted to protect Beru. It wasn't his fault that Xagu had sent me to rescue him.

"Beru Halsted." His name crossed my lips for better or worse.

Svan stood and walked over to the window. His hands turned to fists. I wanted to go after him, but I couldn't move.

"Do you know what will happen if you release that monster?" Svan turned back to me as his lips quivered.

I shook my head no, too afraid to say Beru wasn't a monster.

"If you release Beru, you will bring an evil unlike anything anyone has seen since the Dark wars."

"I refuse to help you further." Svan retreated from the front room, down the hall, and back to the bedroom.

I stood there, confused and conflicted at what I had just been told. Svan being upset with me was unexpected, and now I had no idea how I should feel toward Beru and his part in the Dark Wars. I sat back down, feeling woozy on my feet. Coldness crept into the room, and suddenly it was uninviting.

As I glanced down the hallway at his door, I figured I should leave. But I needed to know more. I had so little information about Beru and desperately wanted to learn more. I pushed my growing feeling for him aside for the first time and committed to doing this fully for Gavin. Perhaps I could talk Svan into helping me without freeing Beru.

Deep in thought, I hadn't noticed that a woman entered the room, one of the ladies in the garden from earlier.

"Svan would like to offer you a room to stay. He is resting now but would like to discuss things at supper with you." The woman stood hunched over in a bow like I was someone of importance.

"Yes, I would like that very much," I accepted his offer with relief. My body sank into the chair and relaxed. We would clear the air at supper, and he would help me get my brother back. Beru would stay in prison, and everything would go back to normal.

I followed the woman as she led me down another hallway to a bedroom.

"May I get you anything?" She opened the door and gestured for me to enter.

"No, I'm fine thanks." I threw my bag on top of the bed.

The woman turned and left me. I plopped back on the bed. It was just as comfortable as Svan's bed. My mind shifted as I thought about how the mattress was made and how Mother would not believe me when I told her how soft it was. It was safer to think of little things than the mountain of mess I had to figure out.

I curled up on the bed, and in no time, my eyes drooped. I was exhausted from the day's events.

Almost immediately I saw the prison with Beru standing in front of me, aware I had dreamwalked.

"I told you not to come back here," Beru barked from where he sat in front of the fire.

"It's not my choice," I scoffed back at him. He was even thinner than the last time I had seen him, if that was possible.

Beru glanced up at me, then flipped over a log for me to sit on next to him.

I hesitated based on Svan's reaction to freeing Beru. I reasoned with myself. If Beru wanted to hurt me, he would have done it by now.

"Or stand. I don't care." He huffed.

I took the seat but moved it a few feet away from him before sitting. Our visits rarely resulted in any new information. He saw me as a nuisance but never questioned me since I was his only company.

"You can't seem to stay away from paradise." He smiled. An infrequent occurrence.

"Only place I know how to dreamwalk to." I picked up a stick he had already broken down so I had something to focus on.

"This wouldn't be my choice," he teased.

"You seem happier when I'm here," I dared to say. He was different when he knew I was around, almost happy.

"Company is hard to come by here, especially the kind that doesn't want to kill you." He poked a stick at the fire.

"What about the other men inside?" I asked, having never questioned him.

"Aria, you can't fix this. No one can." Beru grieved his loss and accepted it.

I held my tongue and didn't challenge him. Even if I had told him the plan, he wouldn't have believed it. If he could be freed, why hadn't it been tried before? My train of thought changed, and I wondered if he knew what became of his family.

"Do you have any family, any messages I could bring to them?" I was on a role to alienate him.

Beru didn't move or speak. He took several long breaths, then stood.

"No." He walked back to the prison.

I got up off my log and walked till I was by his side. I was intrigued to know more about his family, to know if he knew they had been murdered.

"There's nothing you want to know? For me to find out for you?" My hand reached out to him, then I pulled back as I remembered no touching.

He never stopped, just kept walking right to the door.

"So, you just don't care," I called after him, and that caused him to turn back to me.

"I don't care." He turned to me with anger. "I've been here for over two hundred years. Everyone I love is gone."

I regretted my tactics as my plan wasn't to hurt him. His eyes glossed over, and for a moment, I thought he would cry. I thought he would let himself feel emotion. How I desperately wanted to be the shoulder he leaned on, yet I was angry at myself for having the answers he had to be longing for.

"I'm sorry. I didn't mean to anger you. I just wanted to offer you closure," I justified my questions to him.

He remained guarded. I was unsure if he would tell me more about his past or shut me out.

"Do you know about my past?" He half turned to me, his eyes on the ground.

I opened my mouth to speak, but I had no voice. I cleared my throat as I begged for more time before I had to speak. There was no need to discuss his leaving this prison, for it may not even happen, but he did deserve to know about his family.

"Go find out. About me and my past. Then you won't come back here," Beru cautioned.

I stood back as he entered the prison, not bothering to look back at me. My heart sank as his figure disappeared into the doorway. Were my feelings for Beru misguiding me?

I awoke, back in bed at Svan's, and gasped for air. The room had darkened and now smelled of pork being cooked for supper. Had I missed it? I jumped out of bed and opened the bedroom door. The smell of food filled the house. I walked as fast as I could to the front room, anxious to see how late I had been for supper.

As I rounded the corner, Svan sat at the table as he ate his food. He didn't bother to look up at me as I entered and took a seat.

"I'm sorry I fell into a dead sleep," I offered as his servant placed a plate of food in front of me.

"Dreamwalking?" Svan passed me some salt and pepper.

"Yes. I can't help it when I'm overtired." I grimaced, not wanting to make Svan mad again.

"To Beru?" His voice was low, and he filled his fork with food.

"Yes, to Beru. I can't control where I go. I've only ever dreamwalked to the prison." I figured the truth may sway him back over to my side. I needed him to teach me more than ever now.

"Beru had once been the trusted right-hand man of Onen Suun." Svan said between bites. "Did you know that?"

"No, I'm afraid I don't know much about the Dark Wars. Only little things my father told me over the years." I hoped he would tell me more. I placed my fork down to show my interest.

"There are many versions of the Dark Wars. Misconceptions."

"How does Beru fit in this story?" I asked, nervous for his reply.

"Beru should have died as many thought. He's a trickster. Not to be believed."

My cheeks reddened. I shuddered at the thought of Beru working for anything but good.

"Dag'draath works through his lieutenants so he can touch this world," Svan added.

Svan's words stung, as my first instinct was how I had been being played for a fool. I hadn't asked the right questions, but even if I had, Gavin had been my main reason for agreeing to free Beru. I couldn't free someone who could cause harm to our world, but I needed to help Gavin.

"You see the conflict." Svan's voice was stern. He gripped his fork so tight that his fingertips turned white.

"I do," I mumbled with my head down, fearful Svan had seen my selfishness.

I shook my head, unsure how to tame my emotions as I fought against my heart. Could I hold something against Beru he did two hundred years ago? How could he have chosen to risk his life for evil?

"This should be an easy choice," Svan added.

I nodded, however, it wasn't an easy choice for me. There had to be a mistake. Beru wasn't evil. I would have been harmed if he had been. He had never shown any brutality toward me, even when I had been bold. I wouldn't argue with Svan, nor would I tell him my true feelings.

A knock on the door interrupted our conversation. A servant opened the door and brought Sade into the room.

"Sorry to interrupt," Sade said, entering awkwardly.

"You are most welcome." Svan stood and nodded to his servant. "Please join us."

His servant brought over a chair and set a plate for Sade.

"Thank you." Sade sat in her chair and eyed the mass of food on the table.

Her eagerness to eat reminded me she was not used to home cooked meals. She lived on rice and corn. And the odd thing that she could pillage in the woods.

"So, did you get this dreamwalker thing sorted out?" Sade used her hands to shovel food into her mouth.

I placed my hand on my fork that was set on the table and raised my eyebrows at her.

Sade rolled her eyes at me as she picked up her fork.

Svan sat back and motioned for me to answer her question, then he resumed his meal.

"Yes, Svan has been most helpful. I've already learned a lot," I managed to say with a smile. I figured Sade would see through me, but I prayed she had enough sense to wait to ask questions until we were alone.

"These potatoes...." Sade pointed her fork toward her plate.

“Cooked in dandelion oil.” Svan smiled at Sade as he offered her more potatoes.

“That’s it.” Sade shoveled another spoonful in her mouth.

I let out a silent sigh of relief she hadn’t pushed any further. I wasn’t sure how Sade would take the news. Perhaps she would be mad at me for thinking Beru had been wronged. That I was selfish for saving one person and harming others in return. My arms crossed my stomach as it pained in guilt.

“I will leave you both to talk.” Svan stood.

Sade and I stood right after Svan.

“I’m afraid I won’t be able to keep up with you youngsters,” Svan joked as his servant held onto his arm and guided him down the hallway.

Sade and I sat back down and remained silent until his bedroom door closed.

“Spill it.” Sade smiled and leaned toward me as she waited for me to tell her the real story.

“What?” I knew my face would give me away. I was a terrible liar and always had been.

“I didn’t travel all this way to be duped on the good stuff,” Sade expressed.

“Fine.” I gave in. I couldn’t hold out on her, but I dreaded her reaction to what I had just found out.

"There are lots of limitations to dreamwalking. Ones I had no idea about that end in death," I said overdramatically. I hoped stunning her with the thought of me dying would ease her into the news about Beru. She sat and watched me as she nibbled on her food, waiting for more.

My posture sagged, as I told her about Beru.

"And there's something about Beru that came up," I warned, and Sade perked up. "He may have pretended to be on one side but was on another."

Sade's mouth dropped open, and she grabbed my arm. Her eyes dashed back and forth as they matched mine. She was speechless. No quick, sharp comments.

I swallowed excessively. My mouth filled with saliva as my nerves ramped up. I hadn't had time to process today's events, and now I would be getting another opinion of what I should be doing.

"I don't think I have ever been this shocked." Sade cleared her throat several times. "Gavin." Sade grabbed her chest.

It was comforting to see Sade as unsure as I had been. I couldn't risk freeing Beru for my brother now. The danger of setting him free was too great. I couldn't justify risking other people's lives. Now I had to figure out how to save Gavin and stop Xagu and his men from coming after me.

"Time me?" I asked Sade as I lay back on the bed. I'd decided to dreamwalk with the help of Sade.

"How long?" Sade asked as she looked out at the sun.

I shook my head, not knowing how long I could be under, but guessed on past dreamwalks.

"If you see my body in distress, then pull me back." I sounded confident, but I had no idea if this would work to keep me safe.

"Understood." Sade moved her chair over to the window. "Don't do anything stupid." She grinned.

I nodded nervously and tried to fall asleep, I had never dreamwalked on command before. It had always just happened. I willed myself to be back with Beru, uncertain if I should question him or not. I focused on him and what I wanted to say. It wasn't long before I was back at the prison. I tried to hide my grin at my achievement.

“I told you to stay away.” Beru stood in front of me now, his face drawn tight and his voice filled with anger.

“I tried to dreamwalk elsewhere,” I lied. “I ended up here.”

“Why do you keep coming back here, Aria? There is nothing that you can do. This was all decided a long time ago.” Beru lowered his chin to his chest.

Had I opened an old wound with my questions?

Beru opened his mouth to say something but stopped short and turned his back to me.

I’d follow him if he moved. My body tensed as I’d be a fool to think I was safe around him.

“It was a mistake.” I tried to get him to turn back to me. Thoughts of him being a brute were replaced by how kind he had been to me. How happy he had been to see me each time I visited. “You don’t have time to see me?” I called after him. Why was I doing this? I was so confused.

Beru stopped and turned back to me. I couldn’t read his expression. My lips parted, however, no words came out. I couldn’t put two words together while he looked at me that way.

He responded by approaching me—fast.

I didn't have time to think about how to react. He stood close to me, his breath on my face. The heat from his body flushed my cheeks.

"Why are you here, Aria?" He didn't move, his body inches from mine.

I was frozen, barely able to shift my head to the right to avoid his gaze and look toward the ground.

"You don't know me. You don't know this place. It changes people." Beru shook his hand at me angrily. "Leave."

I held back tears, having never seen him so angry before. He was right. I didn't know him. I was a fool to think I would somehow be different to him.

"I won't be back," I shouted after him. I wanted to hurt him like he had hurt me.

Beru didn't say anything. His arms hung by his side, and he watched me almost as if he was willing me to leave.

I closed my eyes and thought about Gavin, Xagu, and the camp. I folded my hands into fists and focused all my energy on being with him. Saving him through dreamwalking.

I opened my eyes, and I was in the woods. Now I needed to figure out where I was. I looked for landmarks that would be familiar. It wasn't long before I knew. It was where I had scouted out the ur'gel camp before I had found Gavin.

I crouched low, unsure if I was visible or not. I didn't want to test it until I found Gavin. I crept to the tent my brother had been held in. An ur'gel came up from behind me I hadn't noticed. He confirmed I was invisible. I forced a huge breath out of my mouth, reassured I could get around easier now.

I walked into the tent, and it was empty. The hair on the back of my neck raised. My nostrils flared as I exited the tent and began my search for my brother in their camp. Xagu better not have lied to me about keeping my brother safe.

It didn't take me long to find him in another tent. It appeared to be his own tent. Relief set in as Xagu did keep his word. While it wasn't up to our standards, it was fit for a royal ur'gel. Snails, their staple food, were in abundance around Gavin, which he was clearly not eating.

I needed to get Gavin to see me, but I still hadn't figured out how to control that part yet. I flailed my arms over my head. Nothing. I held steady and pulled all my energy to my center, visualizing Gavin seeing me. I lifted one eyelid to see if it had worked, but Gavin just stared off into space.

I tried again and thought of how I was able to get Beru to see me. If I could do this, I could get Gavin out of here. I brought my hands up to my chest and visualized Gavin and I leaving together.

"Aria," Gavin yelled as he wheeled his way over to me. "What are you doing here?"

I sent a silent prayer to whatever god had helped me pull this off.

"I'm dreamwalking."

"So, you are one." Gavin sighed as his eyebrows hung low. He was anything but happy for me.

"Yes. But that doesn't matter. I need to get you out of here tonight." I glanced outside of his tent. If Gavin could see me, then the ur'gel would be able to as well.

"What about Beru?"

"That's not going to happen now." I paced the tent as I tried to figure out a way to get us both out of here and realized Sade would be almost ready to pull me back to my body. I couldn't leave Gavin alone in the woods, or worse yet, on our way out of the woods. I needed to act fast.

"They won't stop. I've heard things about Beru," Gavin cautioned me.

"So have I. That plan is dead. We need to move. I need to take you with me back by dreamwalking," I replied confidently as I tried to look like I knew what I was talking about.

"Have you done that before?" Gavin's eyes widened.

"I will tonight." I grabbed his hands and knelt in front of his chair. "I need your energy."

I motioned for him to close his eyes and I held onto his hands with a tight grip. I harnessed his energy with mine and visualized us being back in Western March at Svan's house with Sade, safe.

"What's going on in here?" s voice called from behind me. He startled me, and my grip on Gavin broke.

I flipped around to see Xagu standing there with four other ur'gel, all holding swords aimed at me. I froze, thinking of any potential wounds I could bring back to my own body if they were to attack.

"I'm dreamwalking. I needed to practice if I'm to bring Beru to you. He's not the believing kind," I managed to say, hoping he would believe me.

Xagu, stood at the door and watched us, his body not giving any hints about his thoughts away. Then he raised his hand, and his men lowered their weapons. He turned to them and nodded for them to leave.

"Surround this tent." Xagu stood with his feet apart and his hand close to his sword.

I glanced over at Gavin, who was going along with our story. He was relaxed and calm.

"Gavin is to stay here."

"He's the best one for me to practice on. I have more invested in moving him by dreamwalking than Beru." I stood my ground as I hoped Xagu bought my story.

"You'll only use it on Beru." Xagu didn't move from where he stood.

"I need an emotional connection. I have that with Gavin," I said a little more forcefully than I had been with Xagu before. I worried my time would be limited as Sade got ready to pull me back to my reality.

Xagu narrowed his eyes and remained quiet, then finally said. "Fine."

I nodded to Gavin and got back into the same position. "Focus on traveling with me." I smiled nervously, like I didn't have a lot riding on this.

I held onto his hands and settled into a deep meditation. I harnessed all the energy from the room I could. My hands produced a considerable amount of heat, so much heat that Gavin yelped and pulled back from me.

“What was that?” He shook his hands fast and hard.

“I don’t know. There is no manual with this stuff.” I stood and shook my arms and jumped up and down to regain control. My thoughts focused on Sade and the possibility of my time ending before I could take Gavin. I wouldn’t get this chance again.

“Did you make it to the dreamwalker?” Xagu sat down next to the fire.

“Yes, he’s going to help me.”

“The dreamwalker is going to help you release Beru?” Xagu questioned me.

“Yes.” My focus was on Gavin and not the uncertainness in his voice.

“You told him about Beru?” Xagu asked me again.

“Yes.” I shook my head at him and narrowed my eyes, trying to get a read off his body language.

Xagu stood and walked back to the door. His feet were shoulder width apart, and his sword lay in front of him.

The odd expression on his face worried me. What had I said that would set him off?

"Continue." Xagu nodded at us.

I turned to Gavin, who appeared unsettled and not as interested in the experiment as he had just been. I grabbed his hands, and he flinched.

"I need you to trust me," I warned as I stared in his eyes.

Gavin agreed, and his hand went limp in mine. "Focus on me. Think about the days we played in the barn, bounced in the hay."

"When I could walk?" Gavin snorted.

I needed to make him angry so I could use that energy. I pulled his arms forward, toward me, and settled in again. It was even harder to make this work with another set of eyes as they watched us. Wanting us to fail.

Nothing happened. I let go of Gavin's hands and sat back on the ground.

"I need a minute." Perhaps I had done too much too fast.

"Have you been to see Beru?" Xagu's questions continued.

"Yes, once more," I lied to Xagu again. I kept my head turned away from him so he could not see the deceit on my face.

"You did not tell me," Xagu replied angrily. "I had asked that you send word."

"I didn't make contact with him. He's unaware I had been there."

That part was true. There had been times when I was there and he didn't know.

"You have one more try with this." Xagu waved toward Gavin.

I nodded back that I understood. I would only have one more chance I thought as I stood and wrung my hands out. I pushed the worry and fear out of my mind and put all my focus on Gavin and me.

"Are you ready?"

"Ready as I can be." Gavin glanced over toward Xagu.

"You should leave if this doesn't work," Gavin leaned in and whispered.

"We'll be fine. We both have to be in tune. Can you do that for me?" I asked as my body began to tire.

Gavin nodded, and we got back into position together. I let every thought drift away, and I fixated on Gavin and I being in Western March. Walking around the markets, the amazing food, meeting Svan, and what he would think when he knew Sade had stuck with me. How well he would get along with Astor, and how much more he would pick on me.

Energy zapped in the air all around us and Gavin and I disappeared in plain sight, but only for a short time. I gave it every ounce I had in me.

I heard Sade as she called out to me. My time was limited, and I started to panic. I opened my eyes as Gavin pulled away. He looked past me frightened. I turned back, and Xagu leapt toward me. I fell back on the floor as Xagu fell on top of me.

I opened my eyes. I was back in Western March, in my bed. I turned around to see if Gavin was with me. But all I saw was Xagu standing there, his eyes burrowed deep into me.

"What's he doing here?" Sade had_Xagu cornered in the bedroom with her bow.

"It worked." Xagu examined his surroundings, undeterred by Sade.

I could barely lift my head off the bed as they argued.

"Here, have some of that tea." Sade brought over a cup as her eyes stayed on Xagu.

I took a drink from the mug and almost instantly gained my strength back.

Xagu passed Sade and left the room.

"Where are you going?" Sade called out to him, unable to leave me. "Are you ok to move?"

"Yes, just take my arm." I lifted it up, and she slid it around her neck.

As we entered the hallway, we could see the front door had been opened. We shared a look as we hobbled along.

It didn't take long for things to heat up as the D'ahvol realized that an ur'gel was amongst them. They surrounded us, and I soon realized they considered Sade and I a target as well.

As Xagu reached for his sword, I put my hand on his to lower his weapon as we were outnumbered. I scanned the crowd for Iri, Svan, or Astor.

Xagu pulled me back toward a building as more D'ahvol joined the group.

"You've done it now," I directed my comment to Xagu. He was a natural-born fighter, but this was a death wish.

"Can you get us back to camp?" Xagu kept his eyes on the crowd, waiting for something to breakout.

"No, Sade called me back. If you hadn't jumped me, we wouldn't be in this predicament."

"You lied to me," Xagu stated.

I cocked my head to the side. "How long did you know?"

"When I walked into the tent. A dreamwalker would not have helped you free Beru." Xagu stated.

I shook my head, angry with myself. There was nothing left to do but deal with the current situation at hand.

“I don’t have any weapons on me,” I added.

“My bow is in the house.” Sade stepped beside us.

Xagu turned his head and frowned at me, then he reached under his cloak and pulled out a knife and handed it to me. “This is the best I’ve got.”

“Thank you.” We watched an angry crowd form, and I passed the knife to Sade. “How long do you think we can hold them off?”

“Not long,” Xagu stated. I guessed he wasn’t one for motivational speeches before battle.

“Iri will come. There’s no way this won’t be gossiped about. Most of the city is already here.” I searched the crowd.

“Over there.” Xagu nodded to a booth made from straw. “That’s our best position.”

Sade nodded in agreement.

Xagu passed us as he made a run for the booth, not giving us much of a say in the plan. We followed behind him as arrows flew over our heads, taunting us as we ran.

“They’re a pretty bad shot.” I knelt on the ground.

“If they wanted to hit us, they would,” Xagu stated, his gaze trained on our audience.

"They are clever in battle," Sade added.

I sat back against the building, tired from dreamwalking, and prepared myself to fight for my life if it came to that.

Xagu entered the house behind us.

"We need Iri. He could call this crowd off."

Xagu exited the house with weapons. He handed Sade a bow with some arrows.

Sade readied the bow. "He's not coming. We're on our own."

Sade offered me the knife I had handed to her. I had practiced sword fighting many times, but not up-close combat.

"You'll have one shot. Make it count. Eyes or throat are easiest. The heart is much harder to get to, but if you can do it, they'll go down quick." Sade grabbed the knife and motioned several ways to use it most efficiently.

"We want the big one," someone from the crowd shouted.

Sade stuck her head out and saw one of the men as he stood between the crowd and our booth.

"The big one." The man raised his sword over his head.

“They are calling a one on one.” Sade sat back down and nodded toward Xagu. “They want you.”

Xagu did not hesitate. He stood and assessed the group. He fought almost daily, but the odds weren’t in his favor this time.

“They will want to keep fighting you one on one until.” Sade tested the bow.

“I’m not afraid to die,” Xagu replied in a steady voice.

Xagu put his hands up over his head and walked out into the crowd to meet his challenger. The group behind him cheered louder and hit their spears and shields together. The sound echoed through the city’s core.

“They’ll kill him.” I crossed my arms, unsure of my feelings.

“I’m more concerned if they will stop with him.” Sade stood to watch as the bow swung by her side in her hand.

“What should we do?”

Sade had been here many times before. She knew their customs and rules.

“Wait it out. If there’s a chance to run, I want you to take it. Get to Svan’s house,” Sade stated as her eyes were entranced on Xagu.

Xagu's challenger walked almost all the way around him. The crowd roared for the fight to begin, but both competitors needed to be ready, and a touch of their spears would signal the battle to begin.

Sade and I held our breath as their spears touched.

The challenger stood half the size of Xagu and was quicker on his feet. He danced around Xagu as he tried to pierce him with his spear, missing each time.

"He'll tire out quickly if he lunges at every opportunity." Sade watched the challenger bounce around as he mocked Xagu.

The challenger seemed more interested to please the crowd. The next time he bounced around, Xagu lifted his spear and spun through the challenger's torso. He fell to the ground.

The crowd booed, shocked, unfamiliar with how sturdy and fearless ur'gel were. Another man took his place as the next challenger.

"This could go on forever," Sade stated.

The next challenger wasn't as much into theatrics as the first. The challenger and Xagu walked around each other to try to determine each other's weakness. When they were both ready, they touched spears.

The challenger stayed close to Xagu's body, so Xagu's ability to move his spear became limited. He was also quicker than Xagu and able to cut him several places with quick, short jabs, only enough to annoy him.

Xagu had enough and picked the challenger up by the scruff of his neck and drove the spear through his body. The crowd booed again and yelled for Xagu to die.

Another challenger stepped up, this time female. She made her way to Xagu without any hesitation. They walked around each other, and she spat in his face. When he turned to wipe his eyes, she tried to plunge her spear into his side but failed.

Angered, Xagu stepped back, lifted his arm and pierced his spear through her torso. The angry crowd moved closer to Xagu, and he retreated to our hay booth.

"You're winning them over," Sade said sarcastically.

"Would you rather I die?" Xagu narrowed his eyes at Sade and threw down the new spear he had been handed.

"We can't fight amongst ourselves. We need to keep fighting them off until Iri arrives. We may have a chance." I hoped we could at least work together until then and then get Xagu home.

"He's not due back until the morning." Sade kept an eye on the crowd.

"Try your best to conserve energy," I said to Xagu as he patrolled the booth and waited until he was called out again.

The crowd faced away from us and huddled.

"Seems like they are regrouping." Sade craned her neck to see past a sign.

"They have never seen an ur'gel fight." Xagu pounded his chest, readying himself to go into battle again.

"No, but I get the feeling anything goes here." Sade turned back to us.

"Watch your back," I chimed in.

A horn sounded off, and the crowd parted as the next challenger entered the open space to fight Xagu. He was much taller than the rest, closer in stature to Xagu. He brought a different form of weapon. Two metal balls with spikes connected by a long chain.

"How's he going to fight with those?"

"I've seen that before. If he's good, you're in trouble Xagu," Sade replied. "Keep as far away from him as you can."

"He'll try for my spear with those." Xagu shuddered. It was the first sign of fear he had shown.

"You have more years of experience," I praised Xagu. He needed to keep arrogant. Sometimes that was all you had in situations like these.

Xagu nodded and puffed out his chest as another horn sounded off. He gave us a quick nod and headed back out to fight the next challenger in what would be a long line.

They met in the center and walked around each other, assessing strengths, with the challenger having an advantage in having seen Xagu fight already.

The new challenger lifted his chain and moved his arm in circles. The two metal balls took to the air to show the damage they could do.

"That's not good." I shuddered. It would be easy to grab Xagu's spear in one swing, and he'd be weaponless. "He gave me his knife. His spear is all that he has."

"Shit." Sade's neck flushed.

Sade and I were unable to help in any way. Doing anything would have enraged the crowd and caused more harm to all of us.

The challenger swung his weapon closer to Xagu.

Xagu stood back each time as it nearly reached him.

The challenger swung them lower as he tried to wrap them around Xagu's legs but missed by inches.

Xagu rushed toward him, and the challenger almost lost his balance, causing him to lose the momentum with his weapon. Xagu raised his arm and tried to spear the challenger to the ground but missed. His spear stuck into a piece of wood, and he tried to pull it free.

The challenger seized this opportunity and swung the metal balls into Xagu.

Xagu fell to the ground from the force of metal as it slammed into him. His leather vest ripped as the metal balls tore into his skin. He reached back and pulled the metal ball with its spikes out of his side. He was badly injured.

He held on to the chain with one hand and was able to free his spear with the other hand. As he pulled the challenger toward himself, he sliced his spear into the challenger's heart.

Xagu roared back at the crowd. It was clear the D'ahvol people had underestimated him.

A horn sounded, and Xagu walked back toward us. As he did, someone from the crowd threw a flaming ball of some contraption toward his back, landing about a foot from where he stood.

Xagu's head swung back, and he let out a deep rumbling growl.

The crowd stood back, uncertain of the monster's abilities.

"We don't have much time," Sade yelled from over the stacks of hay.

Xagu retreated into our sanctuary as we assessed his wounds. It took a few minutes as he was covered in blood and badly injured.

"Can you heal me, Aria?" Xagu lay down on the ground.

I had no medicine, and my healing skills were shoddy at best. I placed my hand over the worst wound.

"I only have my energy," I stressed as I got to work. The palm of my hands generated enough heat to begin healing. I used Mother Ofburg's voice in my head to guide me.

Xagu flinched as his wound burned. It was working.

"Hold still." I still had much to learn and could burn his good skin.

The horn sounded off into the distance, and Sade joined us from her watch post.

"Work faster," Sade demanded as a second horn sounded. "The next challenger is up. You're not going to like this one."

I only had time to heal the worst wound. We stood Xagu up and tried to cover his other wounds with fabric to hide them from the next fighter.

"Save that energy for the next round." Xagu patted me on the head as he proudly went back to the makeshift fighting ring.

The next challenger was loaded with weapons. Sword, spear, knife, and other metal objects. He didn't wait for the walk around. He ran toward Xagu to fight. He threw three triangular metal objects with spikes all around them, and they barely missed Xagu.

The challenger swung his sword, and Xagu jumped back as the tip grazed his skin. He smiled at the challenger and brought his spear up, ready to make his kill.

As his spear was up in the air, another D'ahvol appeared behind Xagu and dug a knife deep into his side.

Sade and I gasped as Xagu fell to the ground. His head tilted toward us and he smiled as he fell into his death.

I tried to run out to him, but Sade held me back.

"Let him go. There's nothing we can do now." Sade hung onto me.

Now my worst fear was realized, there would be no one to protect Gavin once the ur'gel learned of their leader's death at my hands.

The D'ahvol carried Xagu's body off in celebration, and Sade and I slipped out from our barrier and found our way back to Svan's as discreetly as we could.

"I need to get to Gavin."

"No way." Sade held her hands up to me. "You just got back from dreamwalking, and you're exhausted."

Sade couldn't stop me. Gavin was in trouble, and I had to bring him through to us tonight. I paced the room as I tried to figure out a plan for it to work this time.

"Word will get back of his death. Then there will nothing stopping the ur'gel from disposing of Gavin." I wanted her more than ever to be on my side right now.

"I won't support this," Sade stated firmly. "You're no good to anyone dead."

As much as I hated she wasn't on board with my plan, she was right. Dreamwalking without having a rest would be very dangerous for both Gavin and me, but I didn't see any other way around it. By morning, the ur'gel would have heard about Xagu's death.

"Wait till morning. You'll still have time before then."

I sat on the bed with my head down. The urge to vomit taunted me, something I was used to when I experienced anxiety. I pushed it deep down inside, but the exhaustion made it difficult to do.

I sprang up from the bed and covered my mouth with my hand, barely making it to vomit into a bucket by the window.

"I'm going to get Svan." Sade turned to run to the door.

"No." I lifted my hand to stop her, and the door slammed shut right in front of her.

"Did you just do that?" Sade stepped back from the door and me as she backed into the corner of the room.

"I don't know." I wiped the vomit off my mouth. Every time I had dreamwalked, my healing and magic abilities had been easier to channel, but my body took longer to recover.

"I think we should tell Svan." Sade knelt beside me and pulled my hair back from my face. "He needs to know."

"Tomorrow. I promise."

Sade took me by the arm and pulled me to my feet. She guided me to the bed, and I plopped down hard. I rolled over on my side and stared out of the window as I waited for Sade to leave me.

"I just need some rest. We'll talk to Svan in the morning. I promise." I didn't bother to face her.

"No dreamwalking till then." Sade lay down on the other side of me.

I lay on the bed and watched as Sade fell asleep. My eyelids burned, but I fought off sleep, until I was sure Sade would not wake up.

I ran through the forest as fast as I could to get to Gavin. I didn't care if anyone saw me.

"It was right here," I said aloud as I came to a clearing where the camp had been. I craned my neck to the left and then to the right. I panicked, knowing they must have found out about Xagu. They had already left for the Western March.

I closed my eyes and held my hands out as I tried to connect with Gavin's energy. There was little time. I inhaled a large breath and concentrated on feeling his energy.

At first there was nothing. Then I sensed someone's energy in the tips of my fingers. I brought my hands to my chest, over my heart. I pulled as much of the energy in as I could. It was Gavin. As I opened my eyes, I was in their new camp.

The ur'gel were unorganized without Xagu. Tents lined too close to each other, no dining hall set up, handmade chairs flipped over and utter chaos. I walked through the camp, unsure if I was visible or not. None of the ur'gel seemed to notice me. It appeared that several of the ur'gel had been fighting over who would be their next leader.

I kept my distance and walked behind each tent to look for Gavin, unsure of how long this cloak of invisibility would last. The first tent I reached had been filled with used boxes and barrels. I jogged over to the second tent, and it had one bed with nothing else in it. I went on, not finding Gavin in any of the tents that had been set up yet. He was here. I could still feel his energy connected to me.

I went to the back of one of the tents so I wouldn't be disturbed. I sat down on the grass and closed my eyes and searched for the right direction to Gavin. It was too dangerous to keep opening tent doors.

I shivered as fear passed through me. Something pushed me to the ground and was beating me. Unable to catch my breath, I rolled to my side to protect myself. It didn't stop. My body jumped as they kicked each rib. My eyes flew open, and I scrambled to my feet as I realized this was Gavin's energy, not mine. I ran through the camp as his energy drew me nearer.

I ran through the core of the camp and came to two female ur'gel who sat in front of a tent. They unpacked several large barrels of food. I stopped when they mentioned Xagu.

"He shouldn't have gone after the girl." The older ur'gel leaned over one of the barrels and pulled out corn.

"Blame Beru. I'm tired of doing all this for him." The younger ur'gel rolled her eyes.

"Don't let anyone hear you say that." The older ur'gel wagged her finger at the young girl.

"At least let us get rid of the cripple." The younger ur'gel sighed.

"The elders will sooner or later." The older ur'gel looked toward a part of the camp that was darkened.

"Sooner the better." The younger ur'gel brought her finger to her throat and swiped it across with a laugh.

I made my way to the spot the older ur'gel had nodded to. It was dark, but I could see the outline of boxes, chairs, and other odds and ends of the camp.

"Gavin?" I called out foolishly and shook my head as he wouldn't be able to hear me.

I moved around the boxes but stopped cold as I heard something behind me. I turned to investigate as the noise got louder. It sounded like something repetitively hitting wood.

I walked over and hoped it was Gavin but also wondered why they would have left him out here all alone. If they hadn't known about Xagu's death, then they should have been treating Gavin as he had asked them to.

As I neared a wagon, I walked around and saw the wheel on Gavin's chair. I breathed a sigh of relief.

Gavin's skin had turned a light shade of blue. He'd been draped in some thin fabric with no other clothes. I searched for something to cover him amongst the boxes but found nothing.

"I'm here, little brother," I touched his hand.

He flinched as he awoke from his slumber.

I stood in front of him and expected that he'd see me since he felt my touch.

Gavin shivered, then cowered as the voice of an ur'gel got closer.

I walked around him to see how the ur'gel had tied him down. There was a piece of rope gathered around one of the wheels of his chair. It had been loosened as if he had tried to get away.

I brought my hands in front of me and cupped them together. As the heat between them formed, I separated my hands by a few inches and shifted my hands back and forth, trying to build a larger force of energy. I closed my eyes and concentrated on building the energy.

"Aria." Gavin beamed as his torso leaned toward me and his arms reached up.

I grabbed him, and we held on to one another, neither of us knowing what the other had been through.

"Are you all right?" I pulled back from him as I looked him over as well as I could with the little light.

"Did he go with you? He just disappeared." Gavin babbled on as I thought of the right words to tell him of Xagu's destiny.

"Yes. I'm not sure how, but he came back with me to Western March." I knelt down so we were face to face.

"That's where they are going." Gavin leaned forward.

"Do they know what happened?" I questioned him harshly. I regretted my tone, but I needed to know everything Gavin knew.

"They know you're a dreamwalker and that he disappeared with you." A ray of light shadowed his face and showed off a large bruise on his cheek.

I grabbed his face in between my hands. "They hurt you."

"We need to leave. Please, take me with you." Gavin sobbed into my shirt to muffle the noise.

"It's going to be okay," I said, not knowing if it would be.

"You can't leave me again. I won't be here the next time you come back."

"What did they do to you?"

Gavin pulled the fabric that covered him off his waist.

I gasped at the sight of the dirty work from the ur'gel. They had seared his flesh.

"Can you heal me?"

"I'm weak." I had little of my energy left. I could either heal his wounds or try to take him back with me. "Once we are safe and I can rest, then I can heal you." I took his hands in mine. "Remember how we tried last time?"

Gavin nodded and replaced the fabric over his cold body. "I'm ready."

As I was about to begin, I heard footsteps off in the distance as they got closer to us. I put my finger to my lips as I hid behind the carriage.

"Who's talking over here?" An ur'gel strode toward Gavin.

"It's just me," Gavin replied.

His voice trembled, and I knew that this was the ur'gel who had hurt him.

The ur'gel picked up a stick and cracked it against the wheel of Gavin's chair.

Gavin jumped but remained staring straight ahead.

The ur'gel leaned behind him and whispered in his ear, "Your time is coming."

Gavin didn't respond. He sat still as he glared straight ahead. The ur'gel walked around his chair, then bent over and pulled hard on the rope and moved Gavin's chair a few feet from the force.

"You stay put." The ur'gel walked away.

I waited a few minutes to make sure that he had left, then raced toward Gavin.

"You okay?" I crouched down to his height to check for any new wounds.

Gavin bent over and fell into my arms, and I rocked him back and forth.

"Xagu is dead," I replied, feeling relief to say it out loud.

"He can't be," Gavin's voice rose.

"He's dead." I nodded my head as Gavin pulled back from me. I didn't need to tell him what that meant for him. He already knew.

"How?"

"The D'ahvol challenged him. He didn't have a chance." The memory of his last smile as he passed over was vivid.

"This will mean war. There are things I overheard." He shook his head as if they were too evil to say out loud.

"We can talk about this later. Let's just get out of here." I took his shaky hands in mine.

"Take all of my energy." Gavin leaned forward, his eyes already depleted with little spirit left.

"I'll take what I need. We can heal later." I pushed his shoulders back straight.

I closed my eyes and took a deep breath in. I pushed the ur'gel and D'ahvol out of my mind and only focused on Gavin and me. I forced myself to only think of us in Western March, laughing, eating, and standing.

I could feel more energy than I had ever before until I touched Gavin. Every ounce seemed to drain from my body. I let go of his hands, frustrated at how little I knew about my own talent and mad at everyone who hadn't told me I was a dreamwalker.

"Behind you." Gavin shook me.

I turned around to see someone as they moved from the shadows of the trees. It wasn't the ur'gel. As the creature came closer to us, the moon hit its cold dark face. Dressed in black, its breath was cold as ice as it hit the warm air.

"Is that what I think it is?" Gavin said quietly.

"It's a dark sorcerer," I managed to whisper. I took my place in front of Gavin, even more aware he couldn't move.

The sorcerer approached at a slow, wobbly pace. A cool mist flowed from its mouth and nose. A hissing sound came from its mouth.

"I keep the boy." The sorcerer walked closer to us.

"He's coming with me." I put my hand on Gavin's shoulder.

"The boy is stuck in place," the sorcerer barked back. "Until Beru is set free." Its head tilted back as it laughed.

"No. I'm taking him tonight," I screamed back at it, not knowing how it would retaliate.

"If you want your brother back safe and sound, then free Beru. The boy won't have much longer." The sorcerer flew off the ground and headed toward us. It disappeared into thin air, inches from hitting us.

I shook my head as I glanced down to Gavin, who promptly said, "Free Beru."

I shot up in bed as I gasped for air. I searched the room as I hoped I had been able to pull Gavin back with me, but it wasn't so. I filled my lungs with air and lay back on my pillow. Not a moment later, I heaved all over the floor.

"Are you okay?" Sade sat up in bed as she rubbed her eyes.

"No." My hands trembled as I waited to vomit again at any second.

"Please tell me you didn't dreamwalk." Sade jumped off the side of her bed and made her way around the bed to me.

My eyes averted to the floor instead of confirming her suspicion.

"Aria." Sade sat on the edge of the bed, careful not to step in my puke, and pushed all the hair off my face.

"I need to talk to Svan." I tried to get out of bed, but Sade pushed me back down and pulled the blanket back on top of me.

"I'll get him," Sade stated as she stood and left the room.

I rolled on my back, worried about the ur'gel coming to Western March and what they would do when they found out that Xagu had been murdered. I closed my eyes as they filled with tears. My heart pounded from leaving Gavin. I let out a sob, and my body shook as I held another one in. I couldn't shake being terrified my brother could be dead next time I saw him. I needed to get back to him.

"Aria." Svan hurried into the room. "What have you done?"

My emotions overcame me, and I sobbed into my blanket. I wished, for once, I had done something right.

Svan sat on the chair beside the bed, visibly tired.

Sade stood at the door as she shifted her weight from one foot to the next.

"Tell me what you did." Svan's lips stiffened into a firm line.

"She's never been like this before." Sade's eyebrows tilted down.

"Dreamwalking can do this. Especially when done frequently, which I expect is the case here. It's hard on the body." Svan waved his hand toward me but averted his gaze.

I lay on the pillow and closed my eyes.

"Let's keep her quiet for a bit." Svan lifted himself up from the chair. "I'm going back to bed. Wake me if she gets worse."

Sade took his place on the chair. "Will she be all right?"

"With rest." Svan placed his hand on mine and squeezed it. "And no more dreamwalking."

Svan's servant entered and placed a bowl with a cloth on a table by the bed. She placed the cold cloth over my eyes.

I rested for a moment. As I heard footsteps go toward the door, I lifted my hand and took the cloth off my burning eyelids. I needed to tell him the ur'gel were coming. I tried to sit up, but someone pushed one of my shoulders down.

It wasn't long before I drifted off to sleep again.

I awoke much later in the day. The sun shined through the window, and wind blew the curtains open. I turned my head. Sade had been sitting on the chair as she watched me. As soon as she noticed I had woken, she got up and sat on the side of the bed.

"How are you feeling?" Sade placed the back of her wrist on my forehead. "Cooler."

"Better." I sat up without feeling the least bit queasy.

"You really screwed up with Svan. I tried my best to fix it, but I'm not sure he'll mentor you anymore."

"Thank you for trying to fix it."

"I tried, but . . . No. I'm with Svan on this. You're not ready to be a dreamwalker. This was really immature."

Her words stung. I had wanted nothing more than to be like Sade.

Sade stood. "I'll get Svan. I'm under strict orders to let him know when you wake up."

I nodded as she left the room. It wasn't long before I relived the events in my dreamwalk. The horror that would ascend on Western March all because of me.

"She lives to tell a tale." Svan clapped his hands together as he entered the room.

"I have something to say." I patted the bed next to me.

Svan stood by the door and ignored my invite.

"The ur'gel are coming. They're looking for Xagu," I said quickly while I had the nerve to confess.

"I have heard about Xagu and figured as such," Svan acknowledged as he stood in place with his hands folded over one another.

"I brought him here, from dreamwalking," I blurted out.

"That I was not aware of, but given your inability to follow rules, I am not surprised."

"I tried to save my brother, but Xagu rushed me. I fell backward. Then I woke up here, and Xagu was with me," I blubbered and hoped Svan would understand. It wasn't my intent to bring Xagu to Western March.

"You must excuse me. I have some cleaning up to do." Svan avoided my gaze as he left the room.

"This is crazy." Sade rushed into the room just as soon as Svan left. "All of the ur'gel are coming to Western March?"

"Yes, I found their camp last night. They know Xagu is here. They don't know he is dead yet," I admitted and waited for Sade to scold me.

"Well, I guess it's a good thing you dreamwalked last night. We'll have a head start on them," Sade chimed as she shook her head.

"I'm the reason that Xagu came here in the first place. This mess is all because of me." I was frustrated at everything that had gone wrong these past few months. Angry for meeting Beru and ever dreamwalking.

"You are." Sade pulled the chair up to the side of the bed and rested her feet on the edge. "But being a dreamwalker is not a choice."

"People are going to die because of me." I choked back more tears.

"Can you stop crying?" Sade rolled her eyes as she wobbled in her chair.

"I can't help being emotional," I said, annoyed at how insensitive she could be at times.

"Then choose not to use emotions," Sade grumbled, moving her head in a circle until she cracked her neck. "It's easier."

"Why?" I pushed.

"What does feeling emotions accomplish?" Sade leaned in, her eyes narrowed.

"That you have a heart."

Sade sat back, unnerved at my response.

I didn't think she was heartless, but that was all I could come up with.

"I know what it's like to lose everyone you love. My family had been murdered right in front of me." Sade shot daggers out of her eyes at me. "You have no right to say that to me."

I shook my head and hated I had gone that far with her.

"You're right. I don't. I'm not myself right now," I confessed to her. I needed her strength and her wisdom.

"For the record, I do cry."

"Over spilled milk?" I tested her with a smile.

"You scared me." Sade hesitated. "I've never been good with friends. I've never had a friend."

"You have at least one." I smiled at her and reached my hand out, and she didn't hesitate to take it.

"Okay, can we get back to fighting now?" Sade joked with me, and we both managed a big belly laugh.

The door opened, and Svan entered. He appeared to be in a cheerier mood.

Sade pulled back, and we shook off our moment together.

"Iri is handling it as we speak." Svan sat down at the end of my bed. "Now, Aria, I want a detailed encounter about your dreamwalk last night. No detail is insignificant."

I nodded and took a deep breath in before I began.

"I went back to the original camp where they had been holding Gavin, but they weren't there. I had been able to pick up on Gavin's energy and found them at a different camp. It wasn't like the other one. It was disorganized and too many ur'gel were fighting to be the leader. They knew Xagu had been in the tent with Gavin and me, and then he disappeared," I spurted out, trying to cover as much ground as I could.

"Where is the new camp?" Svan leaned in.

"Just inside the Lower Forest, before the desert," I replied.

"They're close." Svan was disappointed in my response.

"Is there anything else that has been different than the first trip?" Sade asked.

"There's a dark sorcerer. I had never seen him before. He wasn't acting with the ur'gel." I pondered as I tried to remember what he looked like, but my head hurt.

"A dark sorcerer?" Svan's head popped up from his notes, and his eyebrows lifted.

"Yes. He came from the shadows. It had been difficult to see his face, but he oozed a mist from his mouth and nose, even though it wasn't cold." I shivered thinking of it.

"What did he ask of you?" Svan demanded, his voice quick and his face showing the most interest since meeting him.

"He's holding Gavin, not Xagu. Or at least Xagu thought he had been the one holding my brother." My voice quickened as Svan became more intense.

"Why would he want Gavin?" Sade asked.

"He wants Beru." My gaze drifted to Svan for his reaction.

Svan sat with his chin in hand as he stared down at his paper.

Sade and I were quiet as we waited for him to talk.

"I understand now," Svan broke the silence. He had our attention. "Why they want Beru so badly."

Svan stood and walked over to the window. It had the best view of the desert before Western March.

"Are they coming?" Sade asked.

"Soon." Svan looked back at me. "The dark sorcerers are a group known only as Shadows. They have haunted this area for decades, maybe even longer."

"What do they want?" Sade asked.

"It's been speculated over for many years, but Beru or the prison were never mentioned before." Svan held his finger up, as in a warning.

"What's everyone want with Beru?" Sade sat back down in her seat and tapped her feet on the ground.

"We shall soon find out." Svan turned his back to us as he watched out the window.

"I think it would be a good idea for you to lay low when they arrive. You're weak and might be their target once they find out about Xagu." Sade said, her decision made.

"I have to get to Gavin when they arrive. They are taking him with them." I pulled the heavy blanket off me.

"They won't bring him here," Svan said from the window. "He'll more likely be in a grave."

"They won't kill him." Sade leapt forward and grabbed my hand. "He's too valuable."

"I know they won't kill him," I replied, angered at Svan. "I'll go to him when they arrive. They'll leave him with the women."

"Don't be irrational, Aria," Svan came toward me. "There will be no more dreamwalking."

"I won't need to. They will bring him with them." I lifted my legs over the side of the bed.

"They set up camps close to where they attack," Sade said to Svan as she held out her arms to me as if I was a toddler.

"I'll go with a group of my people, and we will return with Gavin," Svan said firmly.

"Thank you, Svan." I held back tears for Sade.

"There is one condition." Svan's facial expression was stern. "You're not to bring Beru out of prison. No matter what. If you do, it will be nothing like the loss we are about to encounter. This will seem like a speck in the sand."

I only cared about Gavin. As long as I had him back, I could forget about Beru.

Or could I?

"Drinks!" Astor yelled as the barmaid brought our table another round. It was after midnight, and Sade had gone back to Svan's to rest, while I decided to keep Astor company and out of trouble.

"Now, I want the full story on Idok and why he ran from you." I giggled from feeling tipsy.

"I'm testing my boundaries." Astor used an accent. "And I guess they didn't include hair."

"That poor man, Astor. Promise me you won't try to do anything else against him." I couldn't help but laugh.

Astor piped up, "I intend to be on my best behavior. Lesson learned."

I leaned back in my chair as I shook my head and rolled my eyes. I somehow didn't believe Astor.

"Enough about me. Now that Sade isn't here, let's get down with some girl talk." Astor moved his chair closer to me.

"Once a touchy subject, tell me about this love of your life." Astor leaned into me and winked.

"There's nothing to tell." My cheeks flushed, unsure if it was from drink or that the closest thing I had had to love were moments with Beru.

"Those eyes tell me a different story." Astor pushed on the bottom of my glass as I drank.

I slapped his hand away and shook my head at how immature he could be.

"I've never been kissed." I turned my head from him, embarrassed at that fact.

Astor raised one eyebrow. "And I'ma s'posta believe that?"

"It's true." I covered my face and avoided Astor.

"We'll find you love." Astor frowned as he wrapped his arm around my shoulder. He was much drunker than I and would forget whatever I had said tonight.

"That's the furthest thing from my mind right now," I said as I brushed Astor off me.

"Maybe that's exactly what you need." Astor switched my empty glass with a full one.

"Sade told me about your brother. If anyone can get him back its Svan." Astor waved the barmaid over again for more drinks.

"Did she tell you that the ur'gel are coming?"

"Everyone knows about the ur'gel coming." Astor seemed to sober up a little. "The D'ahvol will stop them at the base of the mountain. Don't worry about it."

Astor finished off another drink in one go.

"I almost kissed someone once," I changed the subject and smiled as I remembered the moment.

"What stopped you?" Astor asked.

"Rejection, I guess. Maybe I wanted it and he didn't." I blushed as I shared such a private moment.

"And the kiss?" Astor leaned in for the good bit.

"We almost kissed." I smiled at Astor for his goofiness.

"Just get to the good part." Astor waved his hand at me to continue.

"That's it. An almost moment." I drifted off into the memory of Beru's body mere inches from mine. His sweet scent and how tempted I was to taste his lips.

"So why didn't the kiss happen?" Astor leaned in, enthralled with my little story about nothing.

I grimaced and averted my eyes to the table.

"Did you ever talk about it after?" Astor begged for more information.

"No. It was a onetime thing that I'm not even sure was a thing."

"So, you don't know if he wanted to kiss you." Astor pulled back at his realization.

"No, I mean, I guess." I hadn't thought about what Beru had wanted in that moment.

"Have you seen this person since?" Astor sat back with his drink, his eyes squinted as he tried to piece this story together.

"Yes."

"And..."

A vision of Beru as he sat naked in a bath flushed my cheeks. That had been the next time I had seen him. I was certain he had known I was there, dreamwalking, but he acted like he was alone.

"Let's change the subject. What about you? Any loves?" I prayed he would just talk about himself like he usually did.

Astor smiled and pushed the end of my drink again, but I stopped him.

"If the ur'gel do make it here, I will be of no use to anyone." I moved my glass away from me.

“I think I know who you are talking about.” Astor smiled mysteriously.

“How would you know?”

“You’re not so quiet when you dreamwalk.” Astor winked at me.

“Stop!” I screamed then laughed in embarrassment.

“Oh yes.” Astor hung his head back with dramatics and made me laugh even more.

“Did Sade hear me?” I sobered up at the thought.

“Everyone heard you, darling.” Astor leaned in again and did a double wink.

“Well, nothing happened. If that’s what you’re wondering.” I took a drink from my almost empty glass.

“Except you seemed happier after seeing him.”

I hesitated to share my true feelings about Beru. How I questioned how he was being portrayed. I didn’t feel that Astor would judge.

“I don’t know what to think,” I cautioned.

Astor waited for me to go on.

“He’s just not what I would expect as a Lieutenant of Dag'draath.” I shrugged, not even sure how to put into words how I felt.

"You know him better than anyone, Aria," Astor added.

I did know him better. Others relied on tales from over two hundred years ago. Beru wasn't evil. He was a product of his environment, harsh and isolated. My visits brought out the human side in him.

"I don't feel like I can defend him," I warned. Certainly not to Svan. He wouldn't even hear me out. I'd given in to not defending Beru and trying to forget him.

"I know that you wouldn't like him if he's as evil as everyone says he is." Astor rubbed my back.

"If I tell you something, promise to keep it between us?" I asked as an added backup in case he did remember this conversation tomorrow.

"Always." Astor leaned back and placed his hand over his heart.

I shook my head at his antics. He was a relief in the company I had been keeping lately.

"In my last dreamwalk, I tried to take Gavin back with me, and it should've worked." I swirled what was left of my drink, conflicted if I should tell him what I had seen.

"Yes, and?" Astor's eyes widened as he waited for the punch line in my story.

The image of the sorcerer had been as clear as day in my mind. The way he floated on the grass, the coldness as he had come closer to us. The raspiness of his voice as he taunted me. He was the real "thing" that held my brother back, and Svan was my only hope in getting him back now.

"You can't start a story and stop." Astor waved his finger at me.

I grabbed it.

"Okay, when I visited with Gavin, something came out of the shadows at us." I tried my best to mimic Astor and his theatrics in my drunken stupor.

"Yes?" Astor waited for me to reveal more.

"A dark sorcerer," I yelled, then fell back into a fit of laughter. How was that for an ending?

"Aria, that's not funny," Astor warned, stiff-faced.

"I know." I sat back up straight, self-conscious. Where was the fun-loving Astor now?

"What did it want?" Astor leaned in with a serious look on his face.

"Beru," I replied.

Astor hung his head back and let out a large sigh, and he remained in that position for an awkward amount of time.

He was definitely going to remember this in the morning had been my first thought. The second was I couldn't tell him anything more about my feelings for Beru. I called the barmaid over for another round of drinks to break up the discomfort.

"Thank you," I replied as she placed a pitcher of beer on the table.

"This isn't good. Does Svan know?"

"Yes, he knows everything," I responded.

"Everything?" Astor said.

"Everything except my thoughts on Beru." I laid my arms on the table and put my head down as I felt guilty about my true feelings.

Astor rubbed my back and hugged me.

"You can't help how you feel," Astor whispered in my ear. "No one can change your heart, not even you. It wants what it wants."

I wanted so badly to forget Beru, not to want to free him because I believed he needed another chance. I fought with myself every day to hate him. To forget the conversations we had, the closeness we almost had.

“Let’s get out of here. I’ll walk you back to Svan’s.” Astor got up and pulled at my arm.

Astor paid our tab, and he linked his arm in mine as we left the tavern. The air felt cool, and the city calm. Most of the D'ahvol had likely been on the frontline all evening.

“Your connection with Beru isn’t one you can shake.” Astor matched my thoughts.

“I just can’t help wondering what the missing pieces are,” I added. There had to be something else, a reason he fought for the God of Darkness.

“Have you asked him?”

I shook my head no. I didn’t want to accuse him of anything. I had also hoped to gain his trust.

“No. He wouldn’t have opened up to me as much as he did if I had,” I mused. Maybe I was wrong. What if he did want to set the record straight?

“Then you’re not to blame yourself,” Astor scolded me and pulled me closer to him as we walked.

I needed the comfort of a friendly shoulder. My thoughts drifted back to Noble, as that had been his role in my life. He had been my constant support and knew how to bring the best out of me. I missed that balance. I supposed I could look to Sade for that now.

As we walked to the front of Svan's front door, Astor stopped and leaned in to hug me.

"I think you need one of these."

I hugged him with everything I had left in me and selfishly pretended he was Noble.

"Get some sleep." Astor pulled away from me and waited at the door until I was safely inside, even though I was by far a better fighter than he.

Inside, all was quiet. Svan had left with his crew to find Gavin, and the servants were long asleep. I walked to my room and expected Sade to be in bed, but she wasn't. Instead, she had left a note. *Gone to the frontline. Be back by morning.* I smiled to myself at her dedication and felt guilty for not having gone with her.

I flopped back on the bed, still nervous about the ur'gel advancing, but intent on having a good night's sleep. I needed to feel like myself again. My head was jumbled with random thoughts, some that haunted me. The face of the sorcerer. Gavin being tortured. Beru being the man people were saying he was, and of course, Denny.

I shook my head and tried my best to clear my mind. I didn't want to dreamwalk tonight. I was certain if I did, I wouldn't make it back. I was too damaged. Not to mention drunk.

I rolled over on my side, partially annoyed with myself for wanting to see Beru again, partially not.

"No," I said aloud. I hoped that would reinforce my need for sleep.

I can't see Beru tonight. I can't see Beru tonight. I flipped on my back, stared at the ceiling, and wished falling asleep would come easier tonight.

"I won't dreamwalk," I muttered for reinforcement. I closed my eyes, but I was still awake inside. My body was exhausted, but my brain was running on overtime. Beru claimed my headspace.

I flipped over again, this time hard as if to shake him out. "Just let me sleep," I said to anyone listening. *I mustn't see Beru tonight. Svan will be back tomorrow with Gavin.* I repeated that line over and over until I finally began to drift away.

Tomorrow I would wake, Gavin would be in Western March, and I'd never dreamwalk again.

"It'll be hard for them to get through." Sade walked through the market with Iri and me.

"They'd be fools to try," Iri added as he picked up an apple from a vendor, and the woman flirted with him.

"Do you ever pay for anything?" Sade poked Iri as we carried on down the road and looked for weak links as the city fortified its buildings for a possible attack.

"It's good for morale," Iri huffed back at Sade.

It was nice seeing them get along. Not long ago, they might had been on different sides. Just as Sade had been with the ur'gel. Iri stepped away from us to help a D'ahvol add metal poles to his windows.

"You two seem much more comfortable together."

Sade shrugged it off. "He's okay. But he's not *that* okay." She raised her eyebrows at me as a warning.

“He’s kinda handsome.” I nodded my head toward him.

Sade crunched up her nose.

I laughed and decided not to push this any further. But it did make me wonder who Sade’s type was.

“Over there.” Sade nodded at a young man who struggled to carry materials while wrangling his daughter at the same time. “Can we be of any help?”

“Yes please.” The man dropped his basket and grabbed his daughter just before she almost ran in front of a horse.

“Let me.” I picked up the little girl, who was no more than four.

“She’s a handful.” The man pushed his basket of metal closer to his window.

“She’s adorable,” I said.

Sade knelt over and dug through his basket.

“Are these for the windows?” Sade pulled out the most usable pieces.

“Yes, I’ve gathered everything we had. I’m not sure what would be of most use.”

“Are you alone here?” I tried to keep the little girl entertained in my arms.

"Yes, it's just my sister and me. My father is at the front line. It's grim." The man shook his head.

"They'll hold the line." Sade placed her hand on his shoulder.

Sade turned from me just as I thought I caught a glimpse of a tear.

"I'll take her now." The man took the little girl inside.

"These won't work." Sade knelt again and sifted through the metal pieces. "Too easy to break."

"Not if they are all together." I bent over and picked up pieces of metal and looked at the window for size. I eyeballed it and pieced together a covering.

"That'll work." Sade took my covering over to the window.

I smiled and still hoped Svan would return today with his men and Gavin.

"They should be back soon." I stood and turned toward the direction of the desert.

"He won't make his move unless he is sure he can grab Gavin. It could still be days."

The man came back out of his house alone with more material.

"That's perfect." He put his hands on his knees and inspected my work. "I'm afraid I'm too frazzled to have figured this out myself. I can carry on from here. Thank you."

Sade and I said our goodbyes to the man and headed back down the road to where Iri had been helping another family. As we approached, he walked off to meet us.

"That family set?" he asked.

"They are now."

"How are you doing? No dreamwalking last night?" Sade asked.

"No dreamwalking. I swear." I held my hands up.

"Any connection to Beru?" Sade asked cautiously.

"No. nothing."

"That's a good thing." Sade smiled as she bumped into me. "Right?"

"Yes, a good thing." I forced a grin.

"Iri," someone called from behind us.

We all turned around to see a young boy as he ran to catch up with us. As soon as he was within a few feet from us, he stopped to catch his breath,

"They made it to the front line." The boy's chest heaved up and down as he settled down.

"How bad is it?" Iri stepped out in front of us to ask the boy.

"I wasn't there long before Father sent me back. They are stronger than expected." The boy was visibly shaken.

"What did you see?" Iri leaned down to eye level with the boy.

"They made it through the desert. There's so many. They just keep coming." The boy trembled as he told what he had seen.

"And our men? Were they able to hold them off?" Iri asked as he tried not to pressure the boy too much.

"Yes, I mean, I think so," the boy said with one quick head shake.

"I'll send more men down." Iri patted the boy on his back.

"You run along home to your mother. She'll be worried for nothing. And let's keep this between us." Iri pinched the boy's cheek.

He nodded and took off running.

"The ur'gel are strong. They must know Xagu has died if they attacked." Sade crossed her arms as she watched the boy.

"Or it may be the welcome from our front line," I added.

"We're able to fight from further away. If our men can hold them back, there may be little upfront combat," Iri advised.

Sade and I nodded as we continued down the road.

Iri led as we took a small alley to another part of the city. The buildings in this area were run down, almost forgotten.

"What happened here?" I was confused at how upscale the city had seemed and then this.

"What do you mean?" Iri turned to me, confused.

"Nothing." Sade slapped my arm as she walked past us. "Are you coming?"

"It's just over here," Iri stated as he entered a building. Sade followed him with me hesitantly behind them.

Once inside, it was much nicer. Someone played an instrument in a back room, and it bellowed through the halls. A group of D'ahvol stood around a large table at the back of the room as they leaned over what appeared to be maps.

"Iri." The men appeared happy to see him, then stepped in front of the maps when they noticed us.

"They are with me," Iri said, and the men relaxed.

Iri walked over to the table as Sade and I held back. Iri leaned over the maps and moved some of the papers around.

"We need reinforcements here and here." Iri pointed his finger to several places on the map.

"We have a group ready to leave soon. We can split them up." One of the men took note of where Iri pointed out.

"The ur'gel have reached the line, my friends," Iri advised grimly.

Both men stood back surprised, no other words needed. It was understood what this meant.

"I'll gather more men." The quieter of the men trampled out of the room.

"They're days ahead of us." The man looked back at the map with Iri.

"We mustn't spare anything. The ur'gel can't make it back to our families," Iri stressed.

"Understood. I'll check our stock of weapons and send everything we can," the man said as he started for the door.

"Leave some for the city to use, just in case," Iri called after him. The man stopped just before the door and nodded to Iri before he left.

"You think they'll breach?" I asked Iri, whose back was to me as he studied the maps.

"We can't hold that many men back for long." Iri gazed over the map to strategize.

"Do you want us to stay here or go to the line?" Sade asked.

"You'll both stay with me. They want Aria. We must protect her. If they get what they want, there'll be no Western March or Low Forest." Iri took a break from his maps.

A knock on the door startled us. Iri jumped to his feet to open it.

"I have grave news." A young man stood at the door as Iri waved him into the command center.

"Svan and his team were killed early this morning." He held his hat in his hands and wrung it as he delivered his message.

Time seemed to stand still. Everyone froze as the impossible had happened. Svan was dead, and my only hope for getting Gavin back was gone.

"Are you certain?" I broke from my group, and I grabbed onto his arm.

"Yes. They'd almost made it out with the boy but were attacked in the woods by a sorcerer." The man's eyes were wide and watery.

"Aria." Sade was by my side, but I couldn't lessen my grip on the man.

"Who told you this?" Iri gently removed me from the man and placed me in a chair.

"Moran did, sir. He told me to find you right away to tell you." The man stood at attention as he looked for approval from Iri.

"Did he tell you anything else?"

"Just that you would know what to do. Do you have any messages for me, sir?" the young man asked.

"No. Not now. Go see your family, then return to the line after you have eaten," Iri directed as he walked back to his maps.

"Yes, sir." He turned on his heels and left.

Sade closed the door behind him.

"Svan is dead." I sat in my chair, unable to move.

It took a few moments for us to gather our thoughts and process our loss. The loss of a great dreamwalker who had been advantageous to Western March. One of few left.

"What do we do next?" I stood as I broke our silence.

Iri scratched his head as he leaned on the table.

Sade crouched down in front of the fire. Neither responded.

"There has to be something." I walked to the middle of the room, about to have a meltdown.

Iri took to the map and located where Svan and his crew had been going to rescue Gavin.

"This is the area," Iri added. "Our scout said there were few ur'gel there. Just enough to look after your brother."

"Plus, the sorcerer," Sade chimed in.

"Have you ever fought a sorcerer?" I turned to Iri.

"No. Sade?" he asked.

"Nope." Sade walked over to the map. She leaned over to look at the area where they had Gavin.

"Do you have a plan?"

"I don't know yet." Sade studied the maps. "I've traveled these areas quite a bit over the years. I know I can get us there unseen."

"But?"

"The sorcerer," Sade replied. "That's the missing piece."

"Can we bring Idok?" I grasped at any possible plan.

"He won't leave," Iri stated as he folded his arms across his chest.

"Astor?"

"I like Astor, but this is too dangerous." Sade took a seat at the table with the maps.

"He's not ready for something like this." Iri nodded toward Sade.

"Then who?" I needed an answer. There had to be someone in the Western March that would be willing to fight a sorcerer.

"We'll do it." Iri nodded his head.

"We need someone with magic." Sade plopped down on a chair next to the table.

"I'll find a way. Stay here." Iri headed out into the city.

Sade sat back and lifted her leg to the arm of the chair and swung it back and forth.

I laid my head back on the chair and debated what we should do. It wasn't right of me to ask Iri and Sade to put their lives on the line just so I could get my brother back. If I brought Beru back and he was the man I thought he was, then all this was for nothing. If he was not and he was pure evil, then we were in a worse situation than we were in now.

"I know what you're thinking," Sade interrupted my thoughts.

"What's that?"

"You want to free Beru." Sade kicked up her feet on top of the table, making herself comfortable.

"If he's innocent of what they say, it could be the answer to everything." If Sade agreed, I would be more comfortable in my choice.

"He's in prison because he worked for Dag'draath. You seem to keep forgetting that little bit of information." Sade rolled her eyes as she flipped her head back on the chair to rest.

I wouldn't test her anymore today. I needed to talk to Beru again. To confront him about everything. Then I'd decide if I should bring him back or not.

I slouched down in my chair as I eyed Sade, who had closed her eyes.

I knew what I had to do. Tonight I'd visit Beru and find out once and for all why he fought for Dag'draath.

I marched to Svan's using the excuse I needed food and sleep. As I entered, I went straight to my bed, plopped down, and willed myself to dreamwalk.

Nothing happened.

I sat up and pushed myself back against the bed, angry I still had not mastered the ability to will myself into a dreamwalk. The little voice inside me reminded me I needed to calm down. I had to be in control to dreamwalk. I shook my arms out and relaxed my body by taking several large breaths through my nose and out my mouth.

I felt weighed down. This was a sign I was about to slip into a dream. I put all my attention into Beru's energy and concentrated on being with him in prison. My muscles spasmed, and when I opened my eyes, I was in the prison.

I scoped out the area I first appeared in. Normally I'd be close to Beru, but this time I was alone. I wasn't familiar with this location, but I knew it was somewhere in the prison. I walked down the hallway, cautious of any movement around me. It was grim, the walls painted a dull grey, a hue from the color of the floor. It was windowless, and most of the candles had burned down to their wick's stem.

I caught my reflection on a shiny surface and figured anyone could see me. I needed to be invisible, and there really was no time like the present to practice.

I brought my hands to my chest and thought about my image disappearing in the reflection. I stared at my reflection and concentrated on vanishing. Within a couple of tries, I was no longer visible. I tried to contain my excitement at how quickly I was able to dreamwalk now and control being in both worlds.

I explored the hallways and came across where the prison cells were. The men had been held in small cells, where they showered, ate, slept, and used their chamber pots. They were not in good shape at all. Why had Beru been able to walk about on his own?

After I walked around for what seemed like forever, I heard chatter on the far left of the hall and a familiar voice. As I neared the cell, Beru spoke to two other men.

"Give it to us." One of them threw his hot water at Beru, barely missing him.

"Now." The other man pretended to poke him with a stick.

I stepped into the cell to see what the men wanted. Beru sat on his bed with a plate of food, not enough for a man to survive on, and these men wanted it.

"Take it," Beru growled as he threw it on the floor. "I can't die anyway."

The men scrambled to the floor and grabbed at each piece as they shoved it in their mouths.

Beru lay back down in his bed, not caring who got what.

As soon as they finished, the men left his cell.

It had been a few days since I had seen him last. I had just about lost my nerve to ask him those tough questions, but I reminded myself Gavin was my reason for being here. I had no choice but to get more information before I made my decision.

"I know you're here," Beru said quietly, not moving on his bed. "You can't show yourself in here. It's not safe."

I froze and wondered how many times he had known I had been here when I thought I was invisible.

"Follow me." He flipped his feet over the edge of his bed and stood. He wore only a thin, ripped pair of pants. He reared tall as he stretched his arms out and showed off his lithe, muscular body.

Beru grabbed his white fur and threw it over his shoulders. The only bright thing in his cell. He walked out of his cell and down the long corridor as the other inmates yelled obscenities and tossed their garbage at him. He acted as if none of it happened.

As we reached the door to leave the prison, he pushed it open, and fresh air hit our faces. He walked till we reached the pit where I had visited him before. He got down on his knees and rubbed two sticks together to create a fire. It lit within a few strokes, and he added kindling to the fire.

"You gonna show yourself or just watch me?" He sat back as he waited for me to appear.

I concentrated on him seeing me and managed to transition quickly.

"I told you not to come back here." Beru pointed the stick he had in his hand at me, then tossed it in his fire.

"I came back to tell you why I have been coming here to see you."

Beru didn't move or give much of a reaction. He simply kept watch over the fire.

"Are you interested to know?"

"No. I'm not, Aria. Because it doesn't matter. This is my life, and I'm condemned to it for eternity."

"I need to know why you're here, with them." I pointed back to the prison. He wasn't one of them.

"I'm a prisoner." Beru slid his leg out in front of him, reached down in his boot, and pulled out a piece of bread.

"Why did you give most of your food away? You need it."

"You don't understand how it works here, and I don't care to explain."

The conversation turned sour quickly. I had to get him to see me as a friend. To want to talk to me before I made my decision. I would have to hit him hard with a question he wouldn't like.

"Then explain this. Why did you work for Dag'draath? And how did you get put in a cell?"

Beru grumbled and shifted in his seat.

“Don’t ever mention that name again.” Beru threw a log on the fire.

“You were his Lieutenant.” I stood and wanted to stomp my feet on the ground like a child.

“I was no such thing,” Beru exploded. He stood and walked from me.

“Then tell me why you are here?” I called out to him.

“It doesn’t matter, Aria,” Beru yelled back at me.

“It matters to me.”

Beru stopped but didn’t turn back to me.

I needed him to come back so I could figure out what to do. “Don’t you want your story told? Do you know how many people hate you because they think you worked for Dag'draath?” I wanted him to get mad at me.

Beru turned back. “What do you think?”

“You’re making me think I’m wrong now.”

Beru came back to the fire and sat down. I waited for him to speak first.

“I fought against Dag'draath and his men. I wasn’t one of them.” Beru stared at the fire.

“How did you end up here?” I was confused as only Dag'draath’s people were imprisoned.

"I wouldn't turn on my men. So, they forced me here."

"They didn't find your body, so people think you fought for Dag'draath."

"Well, this has become my life," Beru said. "Scavenging for anything to eat. Because I will live forever."

"And your family? Did they know what had happened?" I hoped he could tell me as much as he knew.

"My family's long gone."

I wouldn't push him on his family. I'd gotten my answers.

I left Beru without telling him much. I needed to get to Gavin, and I didn't have much time before I had to go back to my body.

I found where Gavin was being held. There were only a few ur'gel that had stayed behind to protect the camp so speaking with him wouldn't be difficult. I made myself invisible as I navigated the camp until I found him in one of the tents, laid out on a cot, badly beaten.

I made myself visible and tied the tent door closed. Then I turned to Gavin and knelt at his side.

"Gavin." I prodded his side as I tried to wake him.

"Aria," he managed with a dry mouth.

I noticed some water in a bucket off to the side, dipped my hand in, scooped some up, and brought it to his mouth.

"Here. Don't try to speak just yet." I poured as much as I could into his mouth by hand.

"Have you freed Beru?" Gavin asked with a glint of hope in his eye that he could be going home.

"Not yet, but the plan is in place." I looked over his poorly treated body. "What did they do to you?"

"Don't worry about me. I'll be fine."

I placed my finger to my lips as an ur'gel passed by the tent. The glow from the fire outside showed their shadows inside the tent. I glanced around for a potential place to hide if they decided to enter, but there was nowhere to go. I would have to become invisible in a moment of fear, which I hadn't done before.

After a few tense moments, they moved on.

"I don't understand. They agreed they'd treat you fair." I held my hand over his stomach to try to heal some of his wounds.

“No, don’t heal me. They’ll know you were here, and I’ll get in trouble again. It’s not the ur’gel.”

“Was it the shadow mage?”

“Just tell me you’re going to free Beru. I can’t take the beatings much longer.” Gavin broke out in tears.

I leaned over as best I could without hurting him and hugged him. I fought back the urge to heal. I could sense he had broken ribs. I drew back from him and tried to act strong so as not to upset him anymore.

“I’m going to free him. I need to know where to make the trade.” I sat back on my legs so I could be as close to him as possible.

“There’s a lady. She’s dressed in red. She acts for the shadow mage,” Gavin revealed. “You can leave a message with her.”

“Is the mage here?” I wanted a word with it.

“No. He’s rarely here.”

“Where can I find this woman?” I took his hand in mine and hoped it could offer him strength.

“She’s in the large tent. She’s one of the nice ones. Make sure she is alone,” he added.

“Okay, I’m going to go now, and I’ll be back before I leave.”

"No, I can't risk them knowing you were here to see me." Gavin grabbed my hand.

"I won't come back. The next time you see me, you'll be free." I leaned over and kissed his forehead.

As I turned to leave, he grabbed my arm and pulled me close to him. "Don't come back until I can be free."

I nodded and held back tears at the fright in my brother's eyes. I stood and placed the blanket on top of him so he wouldn't be cold. As I walked to the door, I stopped to blow him a kiss.

I stuck my head out of the tent to see where the ur'gel lurked about. It was well past dark, and most were sleeping by now. I could easily get around the camp being visible.

I crept toward the large tent and waited outside as I tried to listen to the voices inside. I retreated to the woods and waited for someone to leave.

My eyes drooped as I became tired. Just as I was about to fall over from not sleeping, the woman in red left the tent and walked toward the stream. I waited a little bit to see if anyone would follow, and when they didn't, I took my cue.

I followed behind her at a safe distance until she had gone far enough away from the camp so we could talk. As I approached her from behind, she turned to look at me.

"I had wondered if you fell asleep in the woods." She smiled at me then turned back to the stream to fill her pot.

"You knew I was there?"

"Yes. I feel the energy of creatures through the ground." She smiled again. "You came to see your brother."

"I came to leave a message for the shadow mage. I'm told you're the best person to leave that with."

"Yes, that would be correct." She stood there and waited for me to talk.

"I'll free Beru. I need a place and time for the exchange with Gavin."

"I'll pass that along." The woman nodded. It was difficult to believe a person so kind could work for the shadow mage, knowing what it could do.

"Please take care of my brother. I beg of you."

"I try my best to protect him. It's the ur'gel. They don't listen so well." The woman nodded. "You should be on your way. They'll be back soon."

"Thank you," I made my way back to the camp.

I passed by Gavin's tent and forced myself to walk past it. He was lying in there, not chained, and I was unable to take him. It angered me, and the terror in his voice was the only thing that stopped me from going back in his tent with him.

Once everything settled, I would make sure the ur'gel that hurt Gavin would be dealt with.

I grabbed my pack and filled it with anything that could act as a weapon. I had Svan's servants gather up any weapons he had left before his scouting trip.

"You can't go." Sade watched me as I packed my bag.

I ignored her as I stuffed what I could in my almost full sack.

"You're acting on emotions right now."

"He's trapped there, Sade. He wasn't working for Dag'draath."

"You believe him?"

"I do." I stopped what I was doing for a moment to face her. "You don't have to."

"Good, because I don't. You're a fool." Sade grabbed my pack and challenged me.

"I trust him. I can't explain why. We're connected somehow." I tried one last time to get Sade on my side.

"You can't trust him. He's not what you think he is."

"I'll do anything to free him." I grabbed my pack from Sade, but she wouldn't let go. We stood there in a stare off.

"It's not up to me to make up your mind." Sade got up and left the room.

I closed my eyes for a moment and hoped that this would not be the last time I'd see Sade. She risked her life to save mine, and this was how I spoke to her.

I grabbed my pack and my bow, then left the room.

As I opened the door, Sade and Iri stood in the front room.

"You think you can leave without us?" Iri grumbled as Sade stood by his side, avoiding me.

"If you're going to be stupid, then we are coming along. For Gavin's sake." Sade shrugged as she looked toward the floor.

"You're sure about bringing Beru back?" Iri asked.

"Yes. I'm sure. I've thought this through."

"Beru will lead the ur'gel?" Iri had a worried look on his face.

“He’ll stop the attack, I’m certain.” I shuffled my bag on my shoulder.

“I’ll grab my stuff.” Sade brushed past me to get to the bedroom.

“I’m packed and ready to go. We’ll get your brother back.”

I nodded grimly as I thought about what needed to be done for that to happen. While I had made up my mind, I still had questions for Beru. Questions I worried he wouldn’t answer.

“It will be hard once he’s out. He’s been associated with Dag'draath for over two hundred years.” Iri reminded me.

I nodded.

“Ready.” Sade walked out of the bedroom with her pack, bow, and spear. “Let’s go, kids.”

Sade walked past us as she smiled. She lived for fighting.

Iri gestured for me to go ahead of him, and I obliged. As we exited, we turned left and made our way down the mountain.

“Wait for me!” someone yelled from behind us. As we turned around, we saw Astor as he ran toward us.

“Astor?” I yelled, surprised to see him.

"I'm coming with you." Astor proclaimed as he caught up to us.

"Astor, I can't ask that of you. I'm not sure how this is going to turn out."

"You're not asking. I'm telling you I'm coming." Astor struggled to keep up with Iri's stride. "Besides, if I can take out a sorcerer, how interesting would I be?"

Leave it to Astor to still find comedy in a dire situation.

"What about Idok? Surely, he needs you."

"He's rather happy to see me in danger.... I'm trying not to take it personally," Astor replied with a goofy smile on his face.

"You'll have to beat Iri to him." Sade slapped Iri in the chest.

"I don't need any help getting rid of the Sorcerer," Iri said in his gruff, rough voice.

As I walked out of the Western March with the friends I had made on this journey, I was ready for the biggest fight of my life, and I couldn't be prouder of who I'd become because of these people.

"This way. We'll skip around the front and avoid the ur'gel and D'ahvol." Sade veered off into the brush. "Make minimal noise. We aren't equipped to fight a battle."

"So, no road, then," Astor called from behind Sade.

Sade turned back and gave one of her signature looks.

Sade led with Iri behind her, cutting back the brush with his knife, making it easier for Astor and me. The wind picked up and made it more difficult to make our way through without getting nicks and cuts from the branches.

"We'll pace ourselves. We want to make it there when it's dark," Sade asserted as she led us out into a small clearing.

We cut through thick brush for a good part of the day before we decided to stop for a rest.

"No fires here," Iri said to Astor as he collected wood.

"It's too close to the front line," Sade added.

After we dropped our bags and weapons, we took our boots off to get comfortable. My legs were full of scrapes and bruises from the trek.

"There's enough for everyone." Sade passed around dry bread to fill our bellies.

Astor murmured a thank you while Iri inhaled his piece.

"Well, get your last few minutes of sunrays. We should be heading out soon." Sade packed up the rest of the food.

"We'll stop along the way at a farm and get some horses. They will suit us if we have to leave quickly too." Iri jumped to his feet.

We hit the brush again and took a path around the ur'gel. As we got closer to their camp, we took to the woods. Breaking through the brush was the safest route, but it was loud.

Sade dropped to the ground and flagged her arms at us to do the same. She pointed to the north, and we waited for something to happen.

Silence. Had she been mistaken?

Iri crawled slowly a few feet to where Sade had crouched down, and they whispered something to each other. Iri turned back to me and Astor and motioned for us to take cover next to the tree that was closest to us.

We moved slowly to not make any noise with the items we carried. I removed my pack from my back and placed it on the ground behind the tree and got as low to the ground as I could.

Soon we heard them coming. It wasn't a drill. The sound of horse hooves as they hit the ground rumbled toward us.

They screamed and howled as they passed by us. The sound of the branches as they broke reminded me of a hurricane. I held my head down on the ground and hoped they would pass us by.

"Keep going," I heard an ur'gel. Through the woods I'd seen his horse's hooves as they stood still as others ran past.

Why had he stopped?

The rumbling of hooves as they passed by seemed to last forever. Finally, they'd all passed. However, the one remained.

Sade looked back at me and began to rise, but I waved her back down and pointed to the lone ur'gel.

His feet landed on the ground with a thud, and then he walked toward us.

I held my breath.

He stopped only a few feet in front of me.

Silence.

I relaxed at the sound of him relieving himself. He hadn't seen us.

He jumped back on his horse and took off in the direction of the other ur'gel.

"He's the last one." Sade got up from the ground and brushed herself off.

"Let's keep going." Iri walked off into the woods.

"Do you still want to do this?" I asked Astor.

"No going back." Astor walked past me to follow Iri.

Sade led us to the farm Iri suggested, and he secured us several horses.

"There is a shallow bowl of hills not far from here. We'll have the best vantage point from there," Iri spoke as he loaded our packs on the horses.

We left by horse and made it to our destination before sundown. We rounded up the horses and hid them as best as we could.

"Now what?" Iri asked as we waited for the exchange.

"I have to connect with the shadow mage to set up the exchange," I said, unsure of how exactly to do that.

"Did you say mage?" Astor asked.

“Yes, I have to call them somehow.” I looked through my pack for anything I could use to siphon energy with.

“I may be of some help,” Astor offered. “I’ll need some assistance.”

Astor collected rocks and formed a circle with them on the ground. “This is a boundary so the shadow mage can only appear in this circle when called.”

“Sounds good to me.” Sade started gathering more rocks.

“What can I do?” Iri stood next to the circle Astor had started.

“I’ll need some bird feathers,” Astor called out to him, still collecting rocks.

“Get in the trees.” Iri called to us as he ran toward the woods.

We dropped everything and followed him. We all crouched together in a little cave and hid.

“More ur’gel,” Iri said as he peeked out of our hiding place. “They’re at the circle.”

Iri jerked back as if one had seen him. He put his finger to his lips.

I mouthed the word *bow* to Sade, and she pointed to where we had just been.

I was in a better position to see what the ur'gel were doing, I lifted my head to see them as they inspected our belongings and the circle we had just worked on.

They stayed at our site until almost dark. We waited a while before Sade felt we were alone. She then left our cave and scouted our camp to make sure it was safe.

We all crawled out, wary the ur'gel were still close.

"What can I get?" I needed to keep busy as my nerves ramped up.

"Wait." Astor hit his head with his hand repeatedly. "Dandelions, no! Buttercups! Yes!"

Astor appeared pale as he continued to prepare for his spell.

"Are you okay?" I asked, away from the others.

"Yes, Yes," he stuttered as he looked down at his pile of rocks.

"I believe in you." I reached for his arm.

Astor nodded as he placed his hand on mine, then walked past me on his way to grab more items that he needed.

"Are you sure you want him to help?" Sade dropped the items she had collected beside me.

“We just need to support him.”

As I searched for buttercups, I also searched for more ur’gel. That was the second group we had come across. Iri caught my eye as he looked down the hill.

“Everything all right?” I followed his gaze.

“Some lone ur’gel hiding in the woods.” Iri nodded his head to the tree line at the bottom of the hill.

“They’ve seen us?”

“Yes. Been watching us since we came out of the cave.”

“I’ll go tell Sade and Astor.”

Iri grabbed my arm. “Let Astor prepare. He needs his concentration. I’ll keep watch.”

“Are you sure? What if....”

“There won’t be much to do if they decide to attack.”

Guilt hit me hard at the thought of my friends being massacred in order to maybe save my brother. “I’m sorry if this all goes wrong.”

“You have nothing to be sorry about.” Iri grabbed one side of my neck with his large hand. “We sometimes fight for no reason. It’s respectable to battle for good.”

"What are they doing?" Sade interrupted our moment.

The ur'gel had come out from the woods and were now at the bottom of the hill. They stood shoulder to shoulder, a good fifty of them in the line. They all faced us but didn't attempt to climb.

"You said freeing Beru would stop this?" Iri reached for his sword.

"Yes."

"I'm ready!" Astor yelled from behind us, oblivious to the nearby threat.

"You both go. I'll stay here." Iri waved us toward Astor. "Don't let him know."

Sade and I jogged over to Astor.

"Okay, no one goes near the circle because the shadow mage may pull you in, and I can't help you if that happens." Astor sped through the last part of his speech.

"So, I should stay out of the circle?" Sade stepped close to the rocks.

"Well.... they can have you," Astor corrected her.

Sade stepped back from the circle.

"Aria, you're up," Astor took my hand and placed me in another smaller circle below the large circle where the shadow mage would appear. "This is a little something extra for you."

"Why am in a circle?" I stepped over the rock wall onto the buttercup petals.

"As an added bonus, I have you in a protective circle." Astor swung his arms out to showcase his work.

"What about me?" Sade positioned her hand on her hip and cocked her head.

"No one wants us, honey." Astor placed his attention back on me. "Ready?"

"I'm ready," as ready as I could be. The quicker this happened, the sooner we could flee from the ur'gel.

"Stand back." Astor nodded at Sade as he placed a mixture of flowers and herbs he had collected into the circle. Then he gathered a bowl of water and oil and poured it in the circle.

Astor mumbled his spell in a language I couldn't understand any of the words to. The flower and herb mixture took on a form. It spun in a circle as black smoke whirled around. The shadow mage rose up from the ground and stood in front of me. Memories of seeing the creature days ago hadn't prepared me for seeing it again.

"The dreamwalker. You've summoned me, but I see no Beru." Its head spun around without its body moving as it hovered above the ground.

"I'm going to free Beru. We will meet here shortly, and you'll bring Gavin." I tried not to look frightened as this thing grew larger.

"I'll give you till next sundown." The shadow mage vanished into a thick fog as black mist covered us.

"Is it over?" Sade coughed into her arm.

"I think so." I glanced at Astor to confirm.

"It's gone." Astor poked at the circle with a stick.

"They've moved up the hill," Iri said as he approached us. "It won't be long until they're here."

I stepped out of my circle. I had little time to dreamwalk and to convince Beru to come back with me.

I didn't need anything fancy. I lay on the grass and had expected to fall into a dreamwalk like I had the last time. Instead, I lay there wide awake and unable to focus. I straightened myself and squeezed my eyes shut. Still nothing. I wiggled and hoped it would release some tension.

"Um, we don't have much time." Sade knelt down beside me.

"I'm trying."

"Can you try faster?"

"This isn't helping."

Sade stood and walked over to Iri. I watched as they whispered and looked back at me.

I moved my shoulders up and down and cracked my neck. I tried to erase any knowledge of the ur'gel and focused on Beru. I laid my arms by my sides with my palms faced toward the ground.

After several attempts, my body began to sink into the ground, my limbs too heavy to move.

I opened my eyes to find I stood almost in front of Beru. He glanced my way as soon as I appeared.

Beru was hunched over in pain with a large gash on his face and bruised ribs.

“What happened?” I bolted toward him and grabbed his arm just as he began to fall forward.

“It’s just a scratch.” His hand wiped away fresh blood from the side of his mouth.

“Who did this?” I grabbed his face to look over his injuries. He didn’t look well enough to dreamwalk, and I wouldn’t have enough strength to get back if I tried to heal him.

“I didn’t turn over my food fast enough.” He laughed as he brushed off my hand.

“This isn’t funny.”

“I can’t die, Aria.” Beru stood but held on to a tree as he steadied himself.

“I needed you to be in somewhat of a good form.”

“What are you talking about?” He pulled back as far as he could from me.

“I’m taking you back with me,” I promised, aware he’d fight me all the way.

"I'm not going anywhere. Is this why you've been coming here?" He tilted his head up toward me. confused as to why I would want to free him.

"Yes. I'm meant to find you." I pulled a log up and sat down. I had to convince him to come with me.

"What if I don't want to leave? If I've accepted my fate? There is nothing in your world for me," Beru warned as he hung his head.

"You're wrong. You're needed." I leaned in and pleaded with him as I grabbed his hands and pulled him to face me.

"No one needs me."

"If I don't bring you back, they're going to kill my brother." I hoped his sensitive side would give in to me.

"I'm sorry for his death." Beru pulled his hands from me and concealed them under his fur.

"You have a chance to get out of here." I was in disbelief he had been a hero in any regard. He was defeated. "Why wouldn't you take that?"

"What about the rest of them?" Beru warned.

"I don't care about them." I wouldn't leave this dream without him, no matter what.

"I'm still Onen Suun's general here. I have a post."

"A post to get beaten up every day? To have food stolen from you? You're loyal to that?" Could he not hear how unreasonable he had been?

"Lower your voice," he cautioned as he raised his hand and looked back at the prison.

"I don't care who sees or hears me. You're coming back with me."

"These men have been here just as long as I have. At this moment, they don't know they can be freed. I want to keep it that way. Your world is better because we are here," he spoke slowly with precision. "I can't leave this so that you can have your brother back."

"This isn't about my brother. Well, it is, but it didn't start that way," I assured him. "They need a great leader like you."

"Who wants me out?" Beru's eyes narrowed.

I needed to work with this. I had piqued his curiosity.

"Well, the ur'gel and some shadow mage," I advised, fully aware this could damage my case.

"They have your brother?" he asked.

"Yes," I responded as I searched for any hint of him possibly being agreeable to dreamwalk.

"Don't trust them. How do you know your brother is even still alive?"

"I've seen him in a dreamwalk. I have been at their camp. That's when I found out the shadow mage has kept him. I'd thought it was the ur'gel," I offered the truth, hoping that would help me bring him around to coming back with me willingly.

"Oh, Aria." Beru shook his head and let out a large sigh.

"So, you're thinking about it?" I grinned.

"I can't help you." Beru shook his head no.

There was something in his eyes that made me think he'd been trying to convince himself not to come.

"But you can. There's nothing here for you. What are you afraid of?"

Beru stood, angered by my question, and turned his back to me. He didn't walk away, he just stood there and watched the prison. I laid off him for a few moments. I hoped he would come back and agree to come with me.

"What's the worst that could happen?" I demanded as thoughts of my friends being attacked by the ur'gel raced through my mind.

"They could follow us." Beru pointed toward the prison. "Can you guarantee that won't happen?"

"No." I lowered my head in defeat. He had nowhere near decided to come back with me.

Beru grabbed me and pushed me down on the ground. His hand covered my mouth as I tried to wiggle free. He looked off to the side, and I followed his gaze. The prison guards were near.

"They can't find you here. They won't let you go back."

I wrapped my arms around him and hung on as I closed my eyes. This wasn't ideal, but I stole his energy.

"They're coming. You have to dreamwalk," Beru urged as his head flipped between them and me.

"Hug me," I whispered as I kept my eyes closed to concentrate.

"Over there," I heard some call.

Beru wasn't fighting me anymore, and he wrapped his arms around me.

As I opened my eyes, all I could see was the bright light that had surrounded us. We pushed our way through a tunnel. It hadn't been this hard to travel by dreamwalking before. This must have been the prison holding on to us, to Beru. The energy drained me as sadness overcame my body.

I used both of our energies to fight through the tunnel. I couldn't see an end in sight. We had to keep up our momentum until we made it out.

"Is it supposed to be like this?" Beru asked as he clung to me.

"No," I yelled back at him over the noise from the wind.

"It's not going to let us go," Beru held on to me tighter.

"We aren't giving up."

I closed my eyes to help me focus. I needed every ounce of energy from Beru and myself to get to the end of this tunnel.

Lightning sparked as we touched the lining of the tunnel. It jolted us both, and we instinctively let go of each other.

Beru tumbled backward, toward the prison, as I flew in the opposite direction. Once I gained some balance, I moved toward him.

"Focus on me."

Beru held his hand out to me, but without his touch, I could only use my energy. He slipped further away from me.

"It's pulling me." Beru tried to move his body as if he swam, but it was no use.

"Hit the side of the tunnel." I called to him.

"What?"

"Just do it."

Beru held out his legs and arms and rolled into the side. His body jerked back and forth as lightning struck him. He bounced in my direction.

I reached my hand out and our fingers touched, but he was pulled away again.

"Do it again," I yelled as I got closer to him.

He extended his arms and legs again and struck the side even sooner.

This time, I grabbed him and hung on as we hurdled back to the prison.

"Let go of me. You'll make it without me."

"No. We are both going to make it. Hold on."

I dug my nails into Beru's back and hoped his pain could be used for energy.

"Focus on me."

Our speed picked up just a little, but in the right direction. We held onto each other and waited. As we synced, our speed increased.

After several moments of flying through the tunnel, I looked ahead and saw complete darkness. The sounds of dust zapping the tunnel lining became quiet.

"What's happening?"

"I don't know, but it's about to get dark." I tilted my head as I prepared myself for whatever the darkness held.

As we slipped into the black hole, Beru struggled to breathe. I felt his body gasp with each breath as I held him in my arms.

"Not much longer." We drifted aimlessly.

A ball of fire appeared as it whizzed by my head. Seconds later another barely missed Beru.

More appeared as they hit our sides. My skin burned, and energy drained from my body.

"Up ahead."

I looked up to see a gate. "I see it."

Our bodies stiffened, and I forced myself to release the pain and hold onto the energy. We shot forward through the gate that tried to hold us back and landed on the other side on the grass.

"She did it." Astor ran toward us.

“Are you ok?” Sade knelt on the ground next to me.

“Yes. Weak but okay. How is Beru?” I looked over to him as he lay on the ground and barely moved.

“I’ll check him. It’s almost that time. Sade pushed my shoulder back down to the grass. “Rest while you can.”

I nodded as I lay back and closed my eyes.

A chill crept into my bones from the ground as the blades of grass went white with frost. Thick black smoke rolled in like death fog, coming to the edge of our protective circle.

Ur’gel crept out of the trees, their horned heads the only thing I could see above the smoke. My heart raced as I tried to stand. But the fight with the prison had drained me. Still, I staggered to my feet.

The black smoke drifted away, sucked into one place, and formed into the body of the shadow mage.

He was here.

“I got you,” Sade whispered in my ear as she readied her bow.

“The little dreamwalker managed to free Beru.” The shadow mage laughed as his hand reached out from his cloak and gestured for Beru to come to him.

Beru glanced toward Iri, who shook his head no.

Iri threw a sword at Beru, and they attacked an ur'gel. The ur'gel held his ground against the two of them, as they each took a side to attack him on.

Beru swung his sword with expert precision, as he sliced through the thick skin of the ur'gel, but neither Iri nor Beru could manage a kill spot. The ur'gel succeeded to cut into Beru's hand and forced Beru to drop his sword.

As the ur'gel stopped to admire his work, Iri speared the ur'gel in the chest, but not the heart. Iri grabbed the sword Beru dropped and laid it into him, and finally dropped the ur'gel to the ground.

"Thank you." Beru nodded to Iri who just grunted back at him.

"Clever little ones." The shadow mage floated on the ground toward Beru.

"This is my part." Astor smiled at me, and he grabbed a bowl he had hidden behind a pile of rocks.

"You will come with me," the shadow mage said to Beru.

"What do you want with me?" Beru stood his ground as it came close to him.

Astor stood in the background and prepared his potion while Beru kept the mage's attention.

"You'll soon find out." He laughed.

Astor pulled on his black cloak, and with one cast of his hand, the water in his bowl boiled. The smell caught the attention of the mage.

"What are you doing?" He flew at Astor.

"Just a little welcome gift." Astor smiled back at the mage as the bowl lifted off the ground and floated to the shadow mage.

The mage held his hand up and the bowl flew back toward Astor and spilled all over the ground.

"Is that all you have?" The mage taunted him.

Astor waved his hand and another bowl appeared from behind the mage. Its contents soaked him, and he dissolved into thin air.

"It worked!" Astor jumped up with a scream and a fist pump.

"You had no idea if it would work, did you?" Sade asked with more than a hint of irritation.

"There's always the chance," Astor replied as he hunched over to look at the oil left on the ground. "He's actually in there." He marveled at his trick.

"In the oil?" I asked, lifting my head.

"Yes. I'll dispose of it properly, of course," Astor added.

I laid my head back down on the grass just as I heard my name being called.

"Aria!"

"Gavin," I yelled toward the group.

"We'll find him," Beru said as he and Iri took off to the woods.

"We did it, Aria," Sade said as she leaned over and hugged me.

Iri and Beru lifted a battered Gavin out from the woods and laid him next to me on the ground.

"You did it, Aria," Gavin said through tears.

"You're safe now." I rolled over and hugged him. Free at last.

That evening we all sat around the camp fire. Gavin had drifted off to sleep with a full belly, and Astor had gone with him. Iri, Sade, Beru, and I sat by the campfire and finished off our drinks.

"Now what do we do?" Sade asked as she leaned back.

"We plan our next raid." Iri held up his drink, and Sade slapped him.

"What about you, Beru?"

"Eat." He smiled, then placed his hand on my leg. "Then see what this world has for me."

"Lead the ur'gel away from Western March." I moved my leg away from his reach.

"I'll do my best."

"Where will you go, Sade?" I changed the subject.

"I'll stick around for a bit." Sade glanced at Iri, and he smiled.

"And you, Aria?" Beru asked this time.

"I'll take Gavin home. We have a lot of healing to do." I pulled at the grass by my feet as my thoughts turned to Denny.

"They'll be happy to see you." Sade plopped over in the grass and reached for me.

Tears threatened to fall, so I stood. "I'm headed to bed." I turned so no one could see.

I heard a bunch of good nights as I rotated my back just in time. Tears rolled down my cheeks as I headed to where Gavin and Astor slept. Away from the campfire, it darkened, and out of the corner of my eye, I swore I saw a black mist.

Continue reading this series, Legends of the Fallen with book 2, Spell Breaker

https://books2read.com/u/38rjw6

Grab the free prequel to the Legends of the Fallen series, Falling Suun here:

https://books2read.com/u/3R1ElD

Like the series Facebook page to stay up to date on all new releases

https://www.facebook.com/LegendsoftheFallen

Books by J.A. Culican

Novels

The Prince Returns-Keeper of Dragons book 1
The Elven Alliance-Keeper of Dragons book 2
The Mere Treaty-Keeper of Dragons book 3
The Crowns' Accord-Keeper of Dragons book 4

Second Sight-Hollows Ground book 1

Slayer-Dragon Tamer book 1
Warrior-Dragon Tamer book 2
Protector-Dragon Tamer book 3

Spark of War-Through the Ashes Prequel
Sword of Fire-Through the Ashes 1
Embers of Darkness-Through the Ashes 2
Blaze of Magic-Through the Ashes 3

Elemental Origin-Blood of Dragons Prequel
Fire Oath-Blood of Dragons 1

Short Stories

The Golden Dragon-Keeper of Dragons short story
Jericho-Keeper of Dragons short story
Phoenix-Hollows Ground short story
Savior-Dragon Tamer short story
Savior-Dragon Tamer short story

About J.A. Culican

J.A. Culican is a USA Today Bestselling author of the middle grade fantasy series Keeper of Dragons. Her first novel in the fictional series catapulted a trajectory of titles and awards, including top selling author on the USA Today bestsellers list and Amazon, and a rightfully earned spot as an international best seller. Additional accolades include Best Fantasy Book of 2016, Runner-up in Reality Bites Book Awards, and 1st place for Best Coming of Age Book from the Indie book Awards.

J.A. Culican holds a Master's degree in Special Education from Niagara University, in which she has been teaching special education for over 12 years. She is also the president of the autism awareness non-profit Puzzle Peace United. J.A. Culican resides in Southern New Jersey with her husband and four young children.

Contact the Author

I can't wait to hear from you!

Email:
jaculican@gmail.com

Website:
http://jaculican.com

Facebook Author Page:
https://www.facebook.com/jaculican

Twitter:
https://twitter.com/jaculican

Instagram:
http://instagram.com/jaculican

Pinterest:
http://pinterest.com/jaculican

Add me on Goodreads here:
https://www.goodreads.com/author/show/15287808.J_A_Culican

About Tanya Dawson

Tanya Dawson lives in Nova Scotia, Canada with her husband and two Labradoodles - Oscar and Elmer. She wrote her first book in grade five, with the hero decked out in head to toe leather (Oh the 80's!) She is excited to release her first series in 2018 and is looking forward to connecting with her readers.

Acknowledgements

Editor: Frankie Blooding
Cover Artist: Christian Bentulan
Formatting: Dragon Realm Press

www.ingramcontent.com/pod-product-compliance
Lightning Source LLC
Chambersburg PA
CBHW060550310726
48982CB00008B/1075/J

* 9 7 8 1 9 4 9 6 2 1 0 7 5 *